PRAISE FOR THE DE

Here are some of the over 100,000 five star reviews left for the Dead Cold Mystery series.

"Rex Stout and Michael Connelly have spawned a protege."

AMAZON REVIEW

"So begins one damned fine read."

AMAZON REVIEW

"Mystery that's more brain than brawn."

AMAZON REVIEW

"I read so many of this genre...and ever so often I strike gold!"

AMAZON REVIEW

"This book is filled with action, intrigue, espionage, and everything else lovers of a good thriller want."

AMAZON REVIEW

TRICK OR TREAT
A DEAD COLD MYSTERY

BLAKE BANNER

Copyright © 2024 by Right House

All rights reserved.

The characters and events portrayed in this ebook are fictitious. Any similarity to real persons, living or dead, is coincidental and not intended by the author.

No part of this book may be reproduced in any form or by any electronic or mechanical means, including information storage and retrieval systems, without written permission from the author, except for the use of brief quotations in a book review.

ISBN-13: 978-1-63696-014-2

ISBN-10: 1-63696-014-6

Cover design by: Damonza

Printed in the United States of America

www.righthouse.com

www.instagram.com/righthousebooks

www.facebook.com/righthousebooks

twitter.com/righthousebooks

DEAD COLD MYSTERY SERIES
An Ace and a Pair (Book 1)
Two Bare Arms (Book 2)
Garden of the Damned (Book 3)
Let Us Prey (Book 4)
The Sins of the Father (Book 5)
Strange and Sinister Path (Book 6)
The Heart to Kill (Book 7)
Unnatural Murder (Book 8)
Fire from Heaven (Book 9)
To Kill Upon A Kiss (Book 10)
Murder Most Scottish (Book 11)
The Butcher of Whitechapel (Book 12)
Little Dead Riding Hood (Book 13)
Trick or Treat (Book 14)
Blood Into Wine (Book 15)
Jack In The Box (Book 16)
The Fall Moon (Book 17)
Blood In Babylon (Book 18)
Death In Dexter (Book 19)
Mustang Sally (Book 20)
A Christmas Killing (Book 21)
Mommy's Little Killer (Book 22)
Bleed Out (Book 23)

Dead and Buried (Book 24)
In Hot Blood (Book 25)
Fallen Angels (Book 26)
Knife Edge (Book 27)
Along Came A Spider (Book 28)
Cold Blood (Book 29)
Curtain Call (Book 30)

ONE

I was looking through the window at the ash-gray sky. The naked plane trees looked cold, and the occasional, drifting flakes of sleet made them look colder. The search for cold cases on a day like this seemed almost an unwarranted excess. Desultory cars, their headlamps switched on despite it being only eleven a.m., sighed on the wet blacktop. People, muffled like Eskimos, leaned forward as they walked, with their hands deep in their pockets.

It was December. It was December with a vengeance.

Dehan was not looking out the window. She was chewing the butt end of a pencil and frowning at the insides of an old manila file.

"This case," she said without looking up, "was twelve years old last Halloween. We should have a look at it."

I examined the content of my mug and found there was nothing. It was empty but for the dregs. "Why, because it just had its birthday?"

"Cosmic cycles." She looked up, ignoring my bitter humor, and frowned a little harder. "Cosmic cycles," she said again. "Twelve months in the year, twelve signs in the zodiac . . . And also it seems insoluble. Not locked-room insoluble—that's always a hidden hole in the wall—but a genuine puzzle."

I reached out my hand and she tossed over the file. As I leafed through it, she started to recite.

"Sue Benedict, twenty-four, died on Halloween, three days before her twenty-fifth birthday. Sucks, huh?"

"Born in November," I said, scanning the ME's report. "All the best people are."

"Yeah, right. So, her body was found in the bedroom, on the bed, raped, strangled, and stabbed."

"How do we know she was raped and not just killed post-coitus?"

"Abrasions on her inner thighs and around her groin suggest she fought against him. Also, there was a lot of premortem bruising on her neck and thighs, suggesting there was a sexual struggle before he killed her.

"The position of the body on the bed, with the legs spread open, and the bruising from the thumbs on the trachea, suggest that strangulation occurred either during or immediately at the end of the actual rape, while he was still on top of her. He then followed up with what looks like a frenzy of stabbing in the belly, especially around the lower belly. Apparently this is consistent with sexual rage, as it mimics the act of penetration. Semen was fresh and they were able to get a profile. He also left clear finger and thumbprints all over her body, especially her neck and throat. No match was found on CODIS or IAFIS. Swabs and prints were taken from everyone at the party, but no match was found there either."

I put the file down and considered her across the desk, lacing my fingers over my belly. "Suggestive of somebody who knew her, wanted her, but was rejected."

She nodded, then shrugged. The whole thing was a "yeah, maybe" in body language. "It could also suggest a stalker who had been building up a fantasy at a distance. More suggestive is the fact that her windows were all locked from the inside and the door had not been forced. So either her attacker had somehow got hold of a key, or she let him in."

"She had been at a Halloween party..."

"Yup. Seems she was involved in some art group based at the Bethlehem Church hall, near the corner of Lacombe and Thieriot. Had nothing to do with the church, they just rented the hall three nights a week."

I managed to frown and raise my eyebrows in a complicated expression of skeptical surprise. "That's a lot of dedication to art. Usually it's just once a week, isn't it?"

"I wouldn't know, Sensei. Anyhow, this group must have been pretty tight, because they arranged a Halloween party at one of their houses. I think the house belonged to the guy who led the group. On..."

She screwed up her forehead, trying to remember, and I said, "Taylor Avenue, within staggering distance of Sue's house..."

"...On the corner of Patterson. Seems she left the party at about two a.m. A neighbor raised the alarm the next morning. He had seen comings and goings at the house the night before, and when he got up for breakfast, he saw her door was still open."

I sighed. "Art, sex, and a murder, all at Halloween. Edgar Allan Poe meets Georges Simenon. Did you know, Dehan, that turpentine is an aphrodisiac?"

"No, Stone, I didn't know that."

"Yup, that is why you rarely see nudes draped languidly across the beds of writers, but you will often see them in that attitude across the beds of painters."

"Huh. How about musicians?"

"That depends on the style of music, Dehan. Composers and performers in Tudor, Renaissance, Baroque, and classical you will very rarely find with nudes across their beds. However, rock and roll is notoriously sexual."

"Sex, drugs, and rock and roll."

I wagged my pen at her. "In the words of the mighty Dylan, 'Lay across my big brass bed.'"

"Lay across my big brass bed?"

"That is what he said. So what do you say we go and have a look at this church hall and talk to whoever was in charge at the time; see what they can tell us about this bunch of wild, wayward Bohemians?"

She stood. "I say, lead me to the turpentine, Sensei."

It was extremely cold outside. Shards of icy air stabbed through whatever small opening they could find in your clothes and froze small patches of your skin, making your whole body shiver. I looked at Dehan as she stamped across the road toward my Jaguar, with her cheeks flushed pink under a brown woolen hat pulled low over her ears. She was also clapping her gloved hands as she stamped.

We clambered into the car (a burgundy 1964 Mark II, which I had brought with me from England years back) billowing clouds of condensation, slammed the doors, and I turned the key in the ignition. The big, old engine growled and I reversed out of the lot.

It was less than a mile down Soundview Avenue to the Bethlehem Church. As we turned right out of Story, Dehan said, "You know where the mystery lies for me, Stone?"

I glanced at her.

She went on. "The guy knows her. She knows him. That's why she let him in. That's how they come to be in her bedroom with no signs of a struggle. But he makes no effort to hide his DNA. He goes right ahead and rapes her and strangles her. Makes no effort to hide his identity at all. It's like he is super confident that no match is going to be found."

I nodded a lot, chewing my lip. "That is very interesting, Dehan. I agree. It could be the key to the answer."

"And then, he just vanishes. Nobody has seen him, nobody has any idea who he is. He's like . . ."

"Please don't say a ghost. I know it's thematic, with the whole Halloween thing, but don't."

She tried to arch an eyebrow at me, but her woolen hat

wouldn't let her. "I wasn't going to . . . I was going to say a ghoul."

I turned into Thieriot Avenue and pulled up outside a large, white church that looked as though it might have been more at home in a Mexican desert. It was chunky and square in design. The walls were lime washed and there was a giant, wooden cross on the roof above the door. Beyond an iron fence and gate, steps that had been painted oxblood red climbed to an arched wooden door in which two crosses had been cut. To the side of the building there was a large lawn, and at the back I could see a long, low clapboard building, which I guessed was the hall.

The church door stood slightly ajar, like God knew we were coming but didn't want anybody else disturbing his Monday morning with a pot of coffee and the *New York Times*. We clambered out of the car and, as I locked it, Dehan jumped up and down for a bit, billowed vapor from her mouth like a small, woolen dragon, and stamped up the steps to the door. I followed.

Inside, it was dark. Only the golden altar at the far end, beyond the transept, was illuminated. There, candles wavered and reflected off the crucifix, the gilt on the walls, and the frames of the paintings.

We proceeded down the central aisle. I coughed and it ricocheted around the rafters on the ceiling, knocking against the echoes of our footsteps. Out of the shadows beyond the transept, a small man with big eyebrows appeared, as though he'd been dislodged by my cough. He was little more than five feet tall, with a bald, shiny head, brown corduroy trousers, and a sage-green cardigan. He was holding a cloth and a can of furniture wax. The smell was both strong and oddly reassuring.

He looked at us uncertainly, in turn, one after the other, suggesting he was uncertain about both of us. Dehan said, "Are you the guy who takes care of things around here?"

His shoulders rose slowly and his head tilted to one side, like he was shrugging in tai chi. Then he spread his hands: shrugging tiger, uncertain dragon.

"I am not the padre. I am only the handyman." His accent was more Spanish than Hispanic.

I showed him my badge. "I'm Detective Stone, this is Detective Dehan. We're with the NYPD. What's your name?"

"I am Juan de la Torre."

"How long have you worked here, Juan?"

"Twenty, almost twenty-five years. I am naturalize now. I come from Spain . . ." He said "Espaing," but I knew what he meant.

"Do you remember a group of artists who used to rent the church hall, about twelve years ago?"

He nodded. "They still rentin' it. Mr. Giorgio Gonzalez, he is teachin' his classes there, couple of nights por week."

Dehan asked him, "Do you remember the group back then, one Halloween . . . ?"

He was nodding before she had finished. "And the nice woman, Sue, she was kill. I remember. It make me very sad." He pointed back past the transept. "You wanna come in my room? I make some coffee an' you can ask me. Is very cold here in the nave."

We followed him past the altar into the shadows. He pushed open an arched wooden door and led us into a small, neat room with a bed, a small cooker, a table, and four chairs. There was also a single armchair in front of an iron wood burner, and beside it a small bookcase with a couple of dozen books. None of them was the Bible. He saw Dehan reading the spines and sighed.

"I am a communist and an atheist. I told Padre Romero, but he say he don't care. He is a communist and an atheist also. Sometimes he invite me to eat in his house. He is a good man. From Puerto Rico. Please, sit. You like some coffee?"

We sat at the old wooden table and he poured us black coffee. He put a carton of milk on the table and a dish of sugar. We all sipped and he said, "I remember this group. Giorgio Gonzalez is the teacher, back then also. He is Mexican. All the women like him because he has the strong personality, lots of temperament." He gave a small laugh. "I think maybe it is a bit of theater, you know? But he is not a bad artist." He leaned toward Dehan and narrowed his eyes. "Perhaps he is a little bit prisoner of his own culture. You understand what I am saying. He paints like a Mexican in New York. Picasso, Monet, Van Gogh, Goya, they are painting like human beings in the world. Their art is for the everybody. But Giorgio is painting like a Mexican, so he is painting for himself. Is just my opinion."

I smiled. "That is a very good observation. So you said you remember Sue?"

"Yes, of course. She was a nice girl." His face lit up. "Always laughing. Always with a big smile on her face. I like her, and she is always happy to talk. Many people are thinking, 'Oh, Juan is the cleaner. It is no good people see me talking with him.' But no Sue. Sue was off the people. Nice girl."

Dehan asked him, "Can you remember anything that happened around that time that was unusual, that struck you as strange in the behavior of the group?"

He made a face, pulled his mouth down at the corners, and shook his head. "No, the detective ask me the same thing. Nothing . . ." He shrugged again. "Nothing, everything normal, they come in for their lessons, they always laughin', he is teachin' them, makin' a bit of theater, 'Hey, look at me, I am an artist' . . . I remember she was kill on Tuesday. On Monday they have a class and it is a nude girl. Giorgio was jokin' with Sue if she want to be the model. But she say no, and they get a model to come and pose. Pretty girl, nice figure, but *she* was complainin' about the cold. Giorgio was laughin' at her, flirtin', comin' on to her. In the end, I have to go get some more heaters for her because she said otherwise she was leavin'." He looked down at his coffee with a sad face, like coffee just wasn't coffee anymore. "Pretty girl," he said. "Giorgio no respect her."

"Nothing else remarkable happened? Nobody new joined the group? Sue didn't seem different in any way . . . ?"

He shook his head. "No, no, nothin' like that. Everything was normal."

I said, "Who were the people she was closest to, Juan?"

Now he smiled at his coffee. It was a lopsided smile, and after a moment, he looked up and met my eye, then Dehan's. "She like Giorgio. A lot. She use to tell me, 'Oh, Juan, I am crazy about Giorgio! But he don't see me at all! Is like I am no here!'" He laughed. "She really upset when Giorgio was comin' on to the model. I tell her, 'No! You are wrong! He like you, but he playing hard to get. You should be cool with him!' But she don't listen. Until . . ." He paused for dramatic effect. "Fernando join the group."

"Who is Fernando?"

"Fernando Martinez. He is an ol' friend of Giorgio. He is also from Mexico. Women also like him. He is good artist, better than Giorgio in my opinion. So when he is joining the group, Sue is not knowing which way she wanna go: to Giorgio who is ignoring her, or to Fernando who is comin' on strong?"

I laughed. "So what happened?"

He spread his hands, shrugged, and nodded in a way that could only be Mediterranean. "Immediately this happen, Giorgio is all over Sue, and Giorgio and Fernando are competin' with each other for her attention. It was the stupidest thing I ever seen in my life. They was like fifteen-year-old teenagers, you know?"

Dehan drained her cup and set it down on the table, frowning to herself. "When did this happen? How long before she was killed?"

"Oh, very short time, I think like the month before, or two months. I think about it many times because it was sad. He only realize he have to fight for her, when it was too late."

I examined the dregs of black liquid in my own cup for a moment and asked, without looking up, "Juan, did you ever form an opinion about who might have killed Sue?"

He made a long "pfff . . ." noise. "My opinion is only my opinion. You cannot send a man to prison because of my opinion.

But, you know this because you are cops, so this is my *opinion*! People kill for money and sex. I don't know about any money problems with Sue. Maybe she have them, I am not saying she didn't have money problems with somebody! I don't know. I just saying I didn't know about any. But . . ." He nodded a lot, using his whole body. "I *do* know about sex problem, with Fernando and Giorgio. Mexicans, like Spanish, are very jealous people. The night she is kill, she is at a Halloween party with Fernando and Giorgio . . ." He held up his hands like somebody was pointing a gun at him. "You can take out your own conclusions from this. I don't wanna say nothin'. But sometimes, when two men are real close, an' a woman is come between them, they can punish the woman, instead of kill each other."

"Point taken. Was there anybody else close to her at that time that you noticed?"

"Not that I can remember. Better you ask Giorgio. He still livin' here, still doin' the classes."

I looked at Dehan. She shook her head and turned to Juan.

"Thank you, Juan, you have been very helpful. Stay here in the warm, we'll see ourselves out."

As we stood, he watched us a moment. "You openin' the cold case, huh? I hope you get him. She was nice girl."

Dehan nodded. "We'll get him. Don't you worry."

We let ourselves out and closed the door behind us, then crossed the long, dark nave toward the gray, icy day outside.

TWO

It was walking distance, but with the wind picking up and whipping sleet and tiny shards of ice off the East River, and burying them in our skin like frozen shrapnel, we got in the Jag and drove the two hundred yards to Patterson Avenue. Two right turns and another hundred and fifty yards saw us parked outside something that looked like a giant boathouse. It was tall—four stories tall—and narrow: not more than twenty-five feet across. Like many of the houses in that area, it was clapboard, with a long, sloping, gabled roof and tall, narrow windows on the upper floors. There was a garage facing the street on the first floor, and a flight of ten stone steps led up to a kind of veranda at the side of the house and what looked like the front door.

Dehan led the way, still stamping and clapping her hands, picked a path through half-carved hunks of tree, and rang on the bell beside the blue door. It was opened after a couple of minutes by a man in his late forties. What had once been thick, curly black hair was now going gray and thinning on top. He had large brown eyes, a heavy moustache, and gray stubble on his cheeks. He gazed at Dehan a moment like he was thinking there might be an attractive woman underneath all those clothes. Then he gave me a careful once-over, like he was wondering if I would stop him from removing all those clothes. My face and my badge said I would.

"Mr. Gonzalez? Giorgio Gonzalez?"

"Yeah, that's me. Why?"

There was a trace of an accent. I told him who we were, then added, "We'd like to ask you some questions about Sue Benedict. May we come in?"

He sighed. "Sue?" He looked Dehan over a couple of times and stepped back. "Yeah, why not? Come on in."

We stepped over the threshold and directly into a large space with wooden floors and a high ceiling. A fire was burning in a huge, six-foot square fireplace with a bare-brick chimney breast. There were rugs and skins strewn across the floor, heavy linen chairs and a sofa were scattered with careful abandon around the fire, and at the far end of the room there was a massive, wooden table that seemed to be handmade out of raw hunks of tree. Each of the six chairs around it was different, but carefully so. Everywhere there were paintings—some on the walls, others stacked against the walls in reams of five and six—and everywhere there was the smell of turpentine. A giant easel stood near the fireplace, with a large semiabstract nude on it. I stood and looked at it for a moment, thinking how far we had come from Picasso. To him an abstract was an abstraction of form. This was just an ugly distortion of it.

I turned my attention to Giorgio. He was wearing jeans and a T-shirt, and I noticed he was barefoot. Looking at him made me feel cold, but I realized the room was very warm.

He gestured at us, and there was mockery in his eyes, a mockery I figured was habitual. "You can take off your coats. I got triple glazing, and the fire makes a lot of heat, you know?"

He fell onto the sofa, with his arms thrown carelessly along the back, and watched us sit, unbuttoning our coats. His expression seemed to suggest that he was both wise and liberated, and that we drones of the "Establishment" were endemically stupid and did stupid things, like wearing coats in warm rooms. He looked at Dehan as she dragged off her hat.

"You should wear your hair down, *guajira*, it suits the shape of your face, and your neck."

She sighed. "Gee, thanks, Sancho."

A spasm of irritation crossed his face. "What do you want to know about Sue? It was a long time ago."

Dehan spoke, looking at her hat. "How close were you two?"

"You mean was I fuckin' her?"

She frowned hard, still looking at her woolen hat, then placed it on her lap and turned to him. "Is that what I asked you?"

He spread out his arms and crossed his bare ankles, smiling at how stupid the whole damn world was. "I'm just asking. You know, people are usually so scared to talk about sex. They use this crazy euphemisms..."

"What did I ask you?"

"Sure, but I thought maybe..."

"I asked you how close you were. You want to answer the question instead of offering me half-assed theories about social repression? Would that be okay?"

"Woah!" He held up his hands. "Hostile, baby!"

I sighed. My stomach was telling me it was lunchtime and this guy was standing between me and lunch. I said, "Mr. Gonzalez, would you mind answering the question, please? The question was very clear. It doesn't need interpreting. How close were you to Sue Benedict?"

"My apologies, man. Just trying to be clear. She was my private student. I think at one time she maybe had a thing for me. A lot of my students do. We became friends. That was about it."

"What about in the rest of the group? Was there anyone else she was close to?"

His face was a perfect blank, like the question didn't mean anything to him. He gave his head a small shake. "I don't know."

Dehan said, "You met three times a week?"

"Yeah."

"That's a lot of dedication on their part."

"What can I tell you? I'm a good teacher, there was a nice feeling in the class, we had a good groove, you know what I'm saying? We'd put on some music, have a little wine, and paint, man. Paint the night away!"

He laughed and Dehan smiled. "So you had a good rapport with your students. Did they confide in you, discuss their feelings with you? Was it that kind of thing?"

He gave a lopsided smile which you got the feeling he'd practiced a lot in front of the mirror. "Hey, babe, I am just a private art teacher, you know what I'm telling you? You gonna hear some lost souls out there say I got a lot of natural wisdom and insight into people's souls. I did my peyote back home with the shaman, I seen my eagle, but I am just a regular guy who knows how to paint. Maybe..."

I sighed loudly. "Mr. Gonzalez, you're preaching to the choir. I believe you. You convinced me. You are just an ordinary guy, and if I need philosophy, I will go to John Locke or David Hume. Believe me, I won't come to you. We are not asking for insights into anybody's soul. All we want to know is whether Sue had any close relationships in the group, or if anybody was trying to get close to her."

He watched me a moment, shaking his head. "Hey, man, you guys are real hostile, you know that? I invited you into my home, and you're coming at me with this shit."

Dehan stared down at her boots. "Is there any reason, Mr. Gonzalez, why you don't want to answer this very simple question? Did Sue have any close relationships within the group?"

"No." He shook his head and was beginning to look mad. "No reason, and no close relationships."

"What about with Fernando?"

His eyebrows shot up. "Fernando?" He shrugged. "They fooled around a bit, you know what I mean? She liked to flirt, liked to play around, but she was never serious about Fernando. Fernando is a *pendejo*. I love that guy, but you can never take him seriously. He's a player, always on the surface, playing games. He never goes deep, you feel me?"

The question was directed at Dehan, with what he probably thought were smoldering eyes.

I asked, "So there was no rivalry between you and Fernando for Sue's affection?"

He threw his head back, with his arms along the back of the sofa, and laughed out loud. It was too loud and went on too long, so it became almost embarrassing. After a moment, Dehan looked at me and gave her head a small shake. She said quietly, "I was thinking tonight maybe a moussaka? It's so cold..."

I nodded. "Yeah, maybe some prawns and avocado to start, and we could pick up some wine..."

Giorgio stopped laughing but kept a trace of amused irony on his lips. "I'm sorry," he said. "Sometimes the absurdity of people, you know...? People don't understand how I feel..."

Dehan said to me, "Yeah, that sounds good..."

We both turned to look at him. I asked, "You done? So I take it there was no rivalry between you and Fernando..."

He chuckled and shook his head, then affected to make a serious face while winking at Dehan. "No, Detective Stone, there was no rivalry between me and Fernando."

Dehan leaned forward with her elbows on her knees. "Were you aware of anybody in the group who might have had strong feelings for Sue?"

He seemed to think for a while, gazing up at his walls. A couple of times he seemed about to shrug and finally said, "When you say group..."

Dehan flopped back in her chair. I let out a sigh that was on its way to becoming a groan. "It's not complicated, Mr. Gonzalez. Your group of students, or indeed anybody else. Can you think of anybody, either among your students or elsewhere, who might have had strong feelings about Sue?"

He managed to look vaguely pained. "You know, Detective, when I am with my students I am thinking about..." He paused, searching for words, with his hands held up like he was making an offering. "Texture . . . light . . . balance . . ." He gave me a pitying look. "I am not thinking about village gossip, who is fucking who, who has a crush on who . . ."

Dehan sat forward, her face flushed red, but I beat her to it. I said, "Texture? You are interested in texture? Have you ever seen the texture of a tongue when somebody has been strangled? It's like a sponge. And color? The color is a dark blueberry, but it starts to turn to gray after a while. And the face has a weird texture too, like somebody has used a bicycle pump to fill it with water. Kind of bloated and also spongy. Would you like to see the pictures of your friend Sue, after she was strangled, the texture, the color, the balance?"

I sat forward and spoke quietly. "Now, I advise you to listen very carefully to me, Giorgio, because this could make an important difference to your life. Sue Benedict was raped. While she was being raped, she was being threatened with death and possibly mutilation. She must have been terrified out of her mind. Are you capable of imagining what that felt like? After she was raped, the son of a bitch who did it to her then strangled her, and she suffered the most horrific death a person can experience, by suffocation. This bastard then took a knife and went into a frenzy of stabbing all over her belly. Is that enough texture and color for you?"

I paused, examining his face, then went on. "Now, I can see that you don't give a rat's ass about anything that isn't about you. That's fine. But next time I ask you a question, or my partner asks you a question, you are going to give a clear, concise, civil answer. Because if you don't, I am going to drag your sorry ass down to the station house and charge you with obstruction of justice, conspiracy to commit murder, and possession of marijuana and cocaine. You will do time. Have I made myself clear to you?"

At the last couple of sentences, his face had gone a pasty gray and he raised his hands as though I was pointing a gun at him. "Okay, man, it ain't necessary to . . ."

"Don't start."

He closed his mouth and swallowed.

"Do you know of anybody who had strong feelings for Sue, yes or no?"

"No. Fernando liked her, but it was cool. What I am trying to tell you is that, maybe there were things going on in the class and I just didn't notice."

I nodded. "No kidding. Try putting down that mirror sometimes, you might get to see what goes on around you. Can you give us a list of the students you had at that time?"

"Is twelve years ago, man."

"Yes or no?"

He shook his head. "No, I can remember a few people, but not all of them." Then he frowned. "But, you know what? I gave a list to the detective at the time. You gotta have it in your file, right?"

Dehan asked him, "What happened that night? At the party?"

He groaned and rubbed his face with his hands. I noticed they were strong hands and his forearms were corded with hard muscles. He took his hands away from his face and there was an expression of helplessness there. "What happened at the party? What happens at parties. People drink. People dance. We played salsa, rumba, maybe some people smoked dope—not me, I never smoke marijuana!" He laughed. "Sue was tripping..."

I frowned. "On acid?"

"No, man, on the vibe, a natural high. She was dancin', flirting, driving all the guys crazy. She was nice-lookin', you know? Nice body. She was dancin' a lot with Fernando. Then she was givin' me a lap dance!" He laughed a lot. "Sometimes it seems like yesterday. I thought she was gonna stay the night. And Fernando, poor son of a bitch, he was thinkin' he was gonna go home with her and she was gonna fuck with him. But then she told me she ain't feeling so good and she's gonna go home. She tells me maybe I can go over later and wake her up." He made an ugly face and shrugged. "There are plenty of babes at the party, you feel me? I don't need to go chasin' after Sue. I can get fucked right here in my own house. I told her to go to hell and that night I stay with . . ." He gazed up at the ceiling. "Rocio . . . Karen, Karen was from Sweden, and Ruby. They were nice kids." He made an expression that might have been regret. "Next day the pigs . . . sorry, the cops, come around tellin' me Sue is dead. So that's what happened that night."

Dehan thought for a minute. "Any idea where we can find Fernando?"

"Yeah, man. We still hang out. I've known that *pendejo* all my life. He's got an apartment in that cute house above the liquor store, by the public library, on Soundview." He held his hands in front of his face as though he was turning dials. "It's all decorated with zigzag white bricks. I like that house. It's cool."

There was a chime then from the front doorbell. Giorgio hesitated a moment, then stood. As he made his way to the door, I looked at Dehan. She shrugged and said, "I think we're wasting our time. I have no more questions."

I looked up at the ceiling, at the walls, and at the huge fireplace, then at all the paintings. I heard a woman's voice coming from the door.

"I hope I am not interrupting anything. I just made a huge meat casserole, far too much for me, and I thought you might like some . . ."

"Oh, Sandy, that is so generous. You have such a warm soul . . ."

I stood, and Dehan stood with me. They were both looking at us, Giorgio with hostile eyes, the woman with curiosity. She was a youthful forty with a pretty face and a slim, shapely figure which you could see because she had unbuttoned her coat. Her clothes were in stark contrast to Giorgio's: a high-necked blouse with a frill, a string of pearls, a dark skirt, stockings, and high-heeled shoes. Her hair was blond and taken up in a neat bun. She smiled at us.

"I was just saying to Giorgio that I hope I am not interrupting. I tend to cook far too much for myself, and I just *know* that he doesn't look after *him*self! These creative, artistic souls!" She laughed.

I said, "Don't worry, we were just leaving. Are you a neighbor?"

"Sure. I live just across the road!"

"How long have you lived here, Miss . . . ?"

"Beach, Sandy Beach! Can you believe it?" She laughed again, then held Giorgio's arm with the hand that wasn't holding the casserole. "Well, now, let me see. It must be about eight or nine years, or thereabouts."

I nodded and smiled, then turned to Giorgio. "It's narcissistic, your work. Too self-involved. Try looking outward. Enjoy your casserole."

We stepped out into the cold and heard the door close behind us. As we went down the steps, shivering with the icy wind, I felt unreasonably angry. As I unlocked the car, Dehan leaned on the roof and squinted at me.

"Before we go see Fernando, I need some lunch. That asshole made me angry and hungry."

I nodded. "Agreed."

THREE

We picked up a couple of burgers and some fries and sat in the car eating in silence and looking at the freezing world outside. Everybody was either leaning into the wind or hunched away from it. Everybody was padded and had their shoulders up by their ears, and everybody was wearing woolen hats. I said:

"Fernando is just going to tell us the same as Giorgio. Either because it's true, or because he phoned him as soon as we left and told him we were on our way."

Dehan looked at me, a little surprised, and taking small bites of a fry with her front teeth.

"So . . . ?"

"I don't want to go and see Fernando. I want to go and see Rafa Montilla, the detective who had the case to begin with."

"Why?" She shoved the rest of the fry in her mouth with her finger.

"This case isn't just cold, Dehan. It's arctic, like this damn weather. What have we got in the way of witnesses? We have two wiseass artists who wouldn't notice a performing elephant in the room unless it had a photograph of them pasted onto it, and the handyman at the church. Three very limited, very subjective perspectives. We need something broader and more detached to help us choose a line of inquiry."

She nodded into her greasy paper cone. "Okay, makes sense."

While I finished my burger, she called the precinct, got Rafa's number, and arranged to meet him at the Britches Sports Bar on Miles Avenue, in Throggs Neck. It was a ten-minute drive that took almost twenty because I was driving slowly, turning something over and over in my mind. Finally, as we were approaching the bar, I said to Dehan, "You got the list of students there?"

"Uh-huh."

"Bring it in with you. I want to show it to Rafa. I keep going over this. She was killed by somebody she knew, who wasn't there." I pulled up outside the bar, killed the engine, and yanked up the handbrake. "That's wrong, right?"

She smiled and opened the door. "It *was* Halloween, Sensei!"

Rafa was about ten years older than me. He was sitting at the bar with a beer between his forearms, watching reruns of old games and popping peanuts into his mouth. He had a shiny, bald head with long, scraggly hair that hung from his ears to his shoulder blades. When we stepped in, he turned, smiled, jumped down from his stool, and embraced me and slapped my back like we were old buddies. He shook Dehan's hand and kissed her on the cheek. Then he grabbed his drink and he and Dehan moved to a table. I ordered a couple of beers and joined them.

"So," Rafa said, grinning, "you two, huh? Who'd'a thunk it?" He laughed. "No, I'm really happy for you guys." He leaned toward Dehan and gestured at me. "I don't know how you put up with this arrogant SOB, but I am glad for you!"

Dehan gave a small, dry laugh. "You'll say the same to him as soon as I go to the john."

We gave the obligatory laugh, and with the preliminaries out of the way, I said, "Listen, Rafa, you know we're working the cold cases, right?"

"Yeah, I heard you're putting everybody to shame—again."

I shook my head. "Not at all. Cases go cold for very good

reasons. You look at them again with fresh eyes and notice different things. You know that."

"Sure I do. I'm just messing with you." He sat back in his chair with realization dawning on his face. "Ooh . . . So let me guess. You're reopening the Sue Benedict case?"

"Yup."

"Man! After twelve years? I wish you luck. You know me, right? I mean, we were never pals . . ." He turned to Dehan. "Stone and me, we was never like close pals, you know? But he knew me, and . . ." He turned back to me. "You know I would never drop a case unless there was just zero evidence, right?"

I nodded. "I know that, Rafa, and that's kind of why we're here. So far we have three witnesses, for want of a better word. We've Juan at the church, Giorgio, who is a royal pain in the ass and about as useful as a footbrake on a wheelchair, and Fernando, who we haven't spoken to yet, but I'm willing to bet he's going to be about as useful as his pal Giorgio."

Dehan had narrowed her eyes and was shaking her head at me. I knew why and I didn't care.

"Seriously? A footbrake on a wheelchair? You said that?"

Rafa was wheezing a laugh. "Yeah, twelve years ago and you brought it right back. You ask him any damned question and he'd answer by telling you what kind of an artist he was: 'I did not notice, Detective, because me, I am an artist of the soul . . .'"

I laughed. "That's about it. What was your take on the case, Rafa? Did you have any suspects?"

He watched Dehan pull out the list of students and slide them across the table. He shook his head. "Jeez, buy a girl a drink, guys! If you'd given me some warning, I could have refreshed my memory."

He looked over the names, leaned back in his chair, and stared at the TV for a while. Then he started talking while still looking at the TV.

"Things I remember, we went through all the guests, who were pretty much everyone on that list . . ." He paused and looked at me. "You'd know this if you bothered to read the damned report."

I smiled without feeling. "But you have such a nice speaking voice, I like to hear it from you."

"Yeah, right. So we worked our way through them and they all alibied each other, plus we couldn't find anybody with any kind of issue with Sue. But . . ." He reached out and turned his glass around three times. "There were three exceptions to what I am saying: there was Giorgio, who disappeared from the party around two thirty. He says he went up to his bedroom with three women . . ."

"Rocio, Karen, and Ruby."

"Correct."

Dehan had picked up the list of names and was going through them. Rafa said, "You won't find them on the list. They weren't in the group, and they weren't invited to the party. When we challenged him about that, he admitted they were prostitutes and he had called them. He couldn't remember the number."

Dehan asked, "You checked his phone records?"

He shook his head. "By that time, we had the DNA and fingerprints from the lab. Everybody at the party gave us a sample and they were all cleared, including Giorgio. We had no justifiable reason for checking whether he had been with those prostitutes or not."

She grunted, and Rafa went on. "Same thing with Fernando. He said he left with Sue, she told him she didn't want to sleep with him, he went his way, and she went hers. But there is a witness you might want to talk to . . ."

Dehan said, "Patterson Avenue."

"So you *did* at least glance at the report. Yeah, just across the road from Sue. He saw a man matching Fernando's description going up the stairs to Sue's place with her. He said they had a brief scuffle. He went to get the phone to call 911, but when he got back to the window, the man was walking away and the door was closed. Next thing, he saw another man approach and climb the stairs: short to medium height, woolen hat, pretty much nondescript. He saw the door open, the guy stood there for a moment and then went in."

"Could it have been Fernando, come back?"

"That's what I asked. The witness said it was possible, but he didn't think so."

I sipped my beer. "You said there were three exceptions: Giorgio, Fernando, and . . . ?"

"Cyril Browne, with an *e*. My understanding is that he was at the party, though just about none of the people who were there remembered him. Those who did varied from being sure they saw him to thinking they might have seen him. Apparently he's the kind of guy who sits in the corner and nobody knows he's there."

I was surprised and my face said so. "And Cyril was one of Giorgio's students?"

"Yup, and apparently he was pretty good. But in class it was the same as at the party, nobody was ever sure if he was there or not. He never got involved, never spoke to anybody, shy, insecure, whatever. So he was probably at the party, but we can't be one hundred percent sure."

Dehan had been listening with her glass halfway to her mouth. Now she put it down without drinking and said, "Okay, so I am going to ask the stupid question. Why didn't you ask him?"

"He vanished."

Dehan made a face like three Os.

Rafa looked at me and said, "It's in the report."

"We only picked up the case this morning, Rafa. We'll read and digest tonight. Meantime, help me out. What do you mean, he vanished?"

"We went to his house, he wasn't there. We contacted his landlord, he'd given two months' notice end of August, and had left November first."

"The day after the party. That is one hell of a coincidence."

"Tell me about it. Naturally, Giorgio and Fernando were no

longer suspects. Aside from the fact that their DNA didn't match, this guy's behavior obviously made him the prime suspect."

Dehan was nodding. "Did you manage to trace him at all?"

"Kinda. We discovered he had a sister in California. I'm not being funny, but the address is in the file. Elk Grove, if I remember right, in Sacramento. We called her, and she said she hadn't heard from Cyril in years. She said she'd let us know if he turned up. We put out a BOLO." He shrugged and pulled a face. "But it was like he'd vanished off the face of the Earth. We even got a court order to try and recover genetic material from the house, but he'd got professional cleaners in and there was not a trace of him anywhere."

For a moment, he looked embarrassed. "There wasn't a lot more we could do. We canvassed his workmates—he was a librarian—to see if there was anybody who might be hiding him, but the universal consensus was that he was a bit weird, a loner, had no friends, and kept to himself. He'd handed in his notice two months earlier there too, at the same time he handed in his notice to his landlord. Didn't say where he was going, something vague about going abroad."

I called for another round of beers and scratched my head. "So, two months earlier, he decides to kill Sue on Halloween. I get the feeling he is a meticulous planner. He hands in his notice at work and with his landlord, comes along to the Halloween party, and when she leaves, he follows . . ." I paused and shook my head. "I have a couple of problems with this scenario. First, if he is such a meticulous planner, why does he pick a method of killing her that he cannot be a hundred percent sure will work? He can't guarantee she will be alone that night. She might have spent the night with Giorgio or Fernando. Also, even if she was alone, how can he be sure that she will let him in?"

Rafa shrugged. "I'd love to have asked him." Then he suddenly made a face like mental constipation.

Dehan was watching him and nodding like she was reading his constipated mind. She said, "I don't think he's the guy."

Rafa nodded at her.

I said, "What makes you say that?"

The barman came over with a tray of beer and set them in front of us on the table. When he went away, Dehan said, "Okay, this is going to sound crazy, but hear me out. Everything and anything Cyril does is going to look weird and creepy, because the one thing this guy does not want is for anybody ever to notice him. Right?"

Rafa was nodding, staring at his beer. "That's exactly what I think."

I said, "Okay."

"So, the only reason it looks weird that he gave notice at work and to his landlord is because he didn't tell anybody about it. Anybody else would have told his workmates, his family, friends . . . But Cyril is a loner and he doesn't tell anybody. He just goes. So it looks like he's on the run. But aside from the coincidence of dates, there is nothing that points to him as her rapist or her killer."

"Disappearing after a murder is fairly strong circumstantial evidence."

"But did he do a runner?" She raised her eyebrows. "He gave two months' notice. That's not much of a runner. Plus, as you yourself said, the rape has the feel of being opportunistic, not planned. This guy seems to be a planner, not an opportunist."

I grunted. "There is also the small fact of the DNA. He is the only person at the party whose DNA was not tested." I took a long pull and looked at them both. "If not him, who?"

Rafa nodded. "I have to say, Stone, I always thought it was Giorgio. It's wrong to say 'I thought.' There is very little evidence pointing to him, but I had a gut feeling."

"How do you account for the DNA?"

"I can't, but you know like I do, that's not impossible to rig."

I snorted. "Not impossible, but damned difficult."

Dehan gave me a long, skeptical look. "There were apparently three hookers at the party . . ."

I smiled. "So when everybody is good and drunk, Giorgio telephones his three hookers . . ."

Dehan took over. "Meanwhile, Fernando has left with Sue. He makes sure she gets home and returns to the party, where Cyril has been taken into a room upstairs with the hookers. It's all done in the spirit of good fun. The girls are sweet to him and make him wear a condom. Once they have the semen, either Fernando or Giorgio, or both, return, rape, and kill her and plant the evidence."

Rafa leaned back, pointing at her. "I like that theory better than Cyril. It's convoluted because it has to be, but it makes more sense to me as a cop than this little guy planning an opportunistic murder two months ahead. You said yourself, Stone, it makes no sense to plan everything ahead and leave the actual kill to chance."

Dehan's face was almost apologetic. "I have to say I agree. Cyril just doesn't ring true."

I turned it over and around in my head a few times, then asked Rafa, "Anything else?"

He thought for a moment, with his arms crossed, then said, "Basically, Stone, the way I see it, you have three or four options, depending how you look at it. One, like I just said, Cyril planned this murder for at least two months, but left the actual killing to chance; two, and maybe three, Giorgio and/or Fernando killed her and framed Cyril; three, or four, it was opportunistic. Some guy passing saw her go in, saw she was drunk, rang at the door, and pushed his way in."

Dehan drained her glass and tried and failed to repress a belch. "That is in many ways the most likely scenario, but the big drawback is that an opportunist who manages to rape and kill a woman without upsetting any furniture is statistically very likely to have a rap sheet. And this guy did not show up on any database."

Rafa shrugged again. "Which leaves you back with Giorgio or Fernando. Motive would not be impossible to find. By the looks of it, they were into her, but she was not into them. MO? What your partner said. A frame-up."

I gave something like a reluctant nod. "Food for thought."

"I'm sorry I couldn't be more helpful." With a hint of irony, he added, "If I could'a been, I would probably have solved it myself."

I laughed. "Sure. I hear you."

We stood and shook hands, thanked him for his time, and stepped out into the freezing dusk, where the streetlamps and shop fronts were already beginning to light up, and the clouded sky above was turning dark.

"So what now, Sensei?"

I leaned on the roof of the Jag and shuddered. "Now, you get on the phone and request Cyril Browne's financials from the end of August 2006. While you do that, I'm going to phone Frank. Then we go and visit Fernando. We'll see if he's as much of a pain in the ass as his friend Giorgio."

We climbed in the car out of the cold and slammed the doors.

FOUR

Frank's phone rang twice and he answered. I said:

"I am going to frame you for rape and murder."

"You're not normal, Stone. That is not a normal way to start a conversation on the telephone."

I ignored him and pressed on. "So, I am going to lure you into a room with three prostitutes."

"Three, no less, I am flattered."

"They will gather your semen in a condom."

"I see. Are you going to stop soon? I hope you are going to stop soon."

"And I will take that condom to a nearby house, where I will strangle a woman and then introduce the semen into her, making it seem that you raped her."

"I am assuming, John, that this is not a gratuitous threat, but your inimitable way of asking me if such a thing is possible."

"No, Frank, I am threatening you."

"Very amusing, this roughhouse humor. The answer is, it depends. A very astute medical examiner might spot it, but it could just as easily go undetected."

"How would you detect it?"

He sighed and was quiet for a moment. "In the coital,

orgasmic spasm, the man tends to stop thrusting and withdrawing, which is the normal buildup to orgasm, and becomes rigid, pumping, as it were, his semen as deep within the woman as he possibly can."

"You say such pretty things."

"This is nature's way of ensuring that the sperm has the best possible chance of fertilizing the egg. Therefore, if the body has remained immobile since being raped, the bulk of the sperm will have tended to settle mainly in one location, deep within the vagina, leaving only traces elsewhere. However, in the scenario you have described, the sperm would tend to be smeared mainly around the labia, upon insertion, and then along the walls of the vagina. Does that make sense?"

"Indeed it does, Frank."

"What's the case?"

"Sue Benedict, Halloween, 2006."

I heard him scribbling something, then he said, "Would you like me to have a look? It's a long shot, but if it wasn't mentioned in the ME's official report, there may have been some notes or observations on file here."

"Please, Frank. I'd be grateful."

I hung up. Dehan was watching me. I smiled and said, "The big question is, was it pooled at the end or smeared all over? Most MEs would miss it, but our Frank is smarter than most, so he's going to have a look at the notes and see."

"Graphic, but I get the idea. Okay, shall we go see Fernando?"

"Let's do that. After that, I think we have an appointment with a moussaka. This cold is getting to me."

We proceeded through the early dusk, with the headlamps and streetlamps shining hazy through sleet that was gaining confidence and turning steadily to snow, back toward Soundview. Fernando's apartment was above a liquor store beside the public library. Access was via a narrow door to the side of the shop. There were four bells. The top one had his name by it, and we rang.

"*Quien?*"

Dehan said, "NYPD. We'd like to ask you some questions, sir."

There was an audible sigh. Then the door buzzed and we pushed inside. There was no elevator, so we climbed the stairs to the fourth floor. He was standing with the door open, waiting for us. He was about fifty-something and looked as though he worked out at the gym. His hair was thick and curly, and a little too black. He had on a denim shirt over a black vest, and he was clean-shaven.

"What's the problem, Detectives?"

We showed him our badges and I said, "There is no problem, Mr. Martinez. We just need to ask you some questions about Sue Benedict."

"*Susana?*" He gave a bark of a laugh. "Seriously? After all these years?"

"Is that a problem?"

He frowned at me. "No, man. Don't get hostile. I'm just surprised, right? Is a long time."

"May we come in?"

"Sure. But don't hang around, you know what I'm saying? I have a girl coming to watch a movie."

The apartment was comfortable. Giorgio's had been expensive. This was not expensive, but it wasn't cheap either. The furniture was solid and well made, not IKEA, and the sofa and the armchairs were deep and well padded. There was no open fire, but the heavy burgundy drapes were drawn and the apartment was warm. There was a smell of roasting chicken on the air. Like Giorgio, he took the sofa and left the chairs to us.

Dehan leaned forward and asked him, "What can you tell us about the night of the party, Mr. Martinez?"

He laughed. "Not a lot. If I say I was stoned on coke and weed that night, can you arrest me?"

I sighed. "We'd still have to prove it, and that would be almost impossible, and really not worth the effort. We're not interested in that. We are interested in Sue's murder."

"Cool. I was drunk and pretty stoned. What I can remember is that she was coming on . . ." He paused and hesitated. "She was coming on to *all* the guys at the party and some of the chicks too. She was wild that night. To be honest, I was conflicted?" He gave it the intonation of a question, like he was asking us if we understood what conflicted meant. "Because I really liked her? And to be honest, I was hoping we would hook up that night. So, you know, she was kind of wild and open to all kinds of stuff, which was kind of nice. But at the same time I felt like, you know, it's not just me. You know what I mean?"

I nodded. "Sure. How was Giorgio taking all this?"

"Oh, man . . . !" He stared at the ceiling. "That guy is like *the most* arrogant, self-involved, narcissistic prick in the world. I mean, don't get me wrong, I *love* the guy. He is brilliant. But he is so far up his own ass he can look out through his own teeth when he talks. And he was *real* mad at Sue because she was by far the prettiest girl in any of his classes, and he wanted her falling at his feet. And she wasn't. In fact, she was beginning to take an interest in me. So he was like, *what*? You know, like, what the hell is going on here? *I* am God around here!"

Dehan smiled. "So there was some rivalry between the two of you, over Sue . . ."

"But don't expect that macho pig to admit it! I think he even telephoned some whores to come to the party, so he could show Sue that he didn't *care* that she wasn't fawning all over him. Either way, it made no difference because she left the party quite early, about two? Something like that. I mean, it *was* twelve years ago, right?"

"It was, but you are being very helpful, Mr. Martinez, and we are very grateful." She gave him a dazzling smile, which he gave right back. She went on, "So, did you guys leave together?"

"Like I told the first detective, it *must* be in the report! We left together. I asked her if she wanted to hook up, spend the night together, she said no, she was beginning to feel sick and just wanted to sleep. She promised we'd get together in the next day or two and talk about things. I figured that meant we were going to be just friends. So I went home."

I asked him, "You didn't see anybody, a car, a bike, anything out of place?"

He gave a small, sad laugh. "You know, if I had, I would have told you guys twelve years ago."

I nodded. "Of course you would, but you'd be amazed how many people remember things *over* time that they did not remember *at* the time. Mr. Martinez, do you remember Cyril?"

"Little Cyril?" He beamed. "Sure I do! Worked at the library. Sweet guy, but so timid."

"Was he at the party?"

"Oh, sure! I invited him myself. He was class mascot. I loved that guy. I was always trying to get him laid, but he was just so scared of *everything*, you know what I mean? He sat in the corner, with his glass of lemonade, watching, listening. Not talking. He was *crazy* about Sue."

Dehan frowned. "He told you that?"

"Not in so many words, but I used to watch him watching her. And I am telling you, that was pure, unadulterated adoration in his eyes. She was like a *goddess* to him. I used to tell her, go sit on his lap, give him a kiss. But she wouldn't. Sometimes I *made* her? And he would go bright red! But I swear he loved it."

I said, "At the party? Did you tell her to do that at the party?"

"At the party, yes. But I told her in class too, all the time. Jesus! It would have put some fun and light into the poor guy's life. But she was mean. I guess she was a bit of a prick tease. *Always* flirting, but *never* saw it through. I think that made Giorgio pretty mad at her."

"Really? Mad enough to kill her, you think?"

His jaw dropped and his eyes bulged. "Oh, my goodness, *no*! Giorgio is a beautiful, spiritual being. He couldn't hurt *anybody*!

Besides, they found the sperm, right? All the guys at the party were cleared, because the killer left his DNA. That's what *I* understood, anyway." He looked from me to Dehan and back again.

I sighed. "The case isn't closed, Mr. Martinez, and until it's closed, every avenue remains a possibility."

"Gosh," he said. "I see. Do I need a lawyer, then?"

Dehan smiled like she was going to reassure him, but said, "I don't know, do you?"

He sat up straight, half laughing. "Well, you're making me nervous! Of course not. We all loved Sue, some of us more than others, but we all loved her. You know what I think? I think she was so drunk she left the door open, and some passing punk saw it, went in, and killed the poor child. She was so gorgeous!"

I saw Dehan's eyes narrow and she drew breath. I knew what she was going to ask him, but I cut across her. "You may well be right, Mr. Martinez." I looked at Dehan and told her with my face not to pursue it. "Tell me, how long have you and Giorgio been friends?"

"Oh, my God! Since we were kids. We grew up on the same street in Chihuahua. Even our fathers were friends. You know what I'm saying? We came to U.S.A. together, we did everything together. We go back a long way. I criticize him? I call him names? But we are real tight, and there for each other, come what may."

I watched him closely a moment and realized he was older than I had thought. I smiled. "Like brothers, huh? Stick by each other through thick and thin. That's nice. More people should be like that."

He seemed uncertain, but pleased, and said, "I *know*, right?"

I stood. "Mr. Martinez, thank you very much for your help and cooperation. I am sorry to have taken up your time. I hope you have a very pleasant evening with your date."

"Thank you, Detective." He stood too, and so did Dehan. "I wish all NYPD officers were as courteous as you two. You have a lovely evening too, y'hear!"

He let us out, and as Dehan followed me down the stairs, I heard the door close behind us. We stepped out into the dark, freezing street and walked to the car. That was when Dehan said, "You want to tell me what that was all about, partner?"

I nodded. "Sorry. I didn't want to go there yet. He clearly doesn't know a witness saw him with Sue at her door. Let's keep it that way for now. I need a few hours to get a handle on this. There is something very, very wrong here."

She looked at me curiously. "What do you mean?"

I shook my head. "I don't know yet. Moussaka, Dehan. Moussaka and wine. And let me think."

I threw her the keys and climbed in the passenger seat. The doors slammed, the engine growled, and we pulled out into the slow stream of traffic on Soundview Avenue. The wipers set up a slow, steady squeak and thud, pushing the melting flakes of sleet from the windshield. I leaned against the door with my head on the cold window and watched the people hurrying through the frosted, pre-Christmas light. After a while, Dehan frowned at me.

"Was it my imagination, or is Fernando gay?"

I grunted. "I don't know if he's gay, but it wasn't your imagination."

"Huh?"

I laughed a small laugh. "He is a little camp, affected, but he might still like, or even prefer, women."

She nodded and made a face. "Okay . . ."

"Sex is complicated . . ."

I said it half to myself, but she turned and smiled a smile that was full of promise and warmth and said, "No, it's not."

"Keep your eyes on the road, you wonton hussy." I rubbed my face with the palms of my hands. "We have every reason to believe she knew her killer. We will confirm that tomorrow, but as a working hypothesis, which we can be pretty sure of, we can say for now that we have every reason to believe that she knew her killer. A, because there was no sign of a forced entry, and B, because we have a witness whom we shall speak to tomorrow, who saw a man climb the steps, knock on the door, and go in. That makes it very unlikely it was a passerby. Agreed?"

"Agreed."

"So, for now at least, this narrows our pool to Giorgio, Fernando, and Cyril, none of whom is completely convincing. You like both Giorgio and Fernando . . ."

"And," she interrupted me, "you didn't let me press him on it, but note that Fernando lied about going home. He said they parted company when they left the party, but he went home with her, and we don't know if he went inside. Like you say, we will talk to the witness tomorrow, but that second man who went in could have been Fernando *or* Giorgio. Agreed?"

I was quiet for a bit, then nodded. "Agreed."

"And if he is gay, or part gay or whatever, the three of them could have had some weird sex thing going on, some kind of Sharon Tate shit."

I shook my head and sighed. "Dehan, I don't know how to even begin to answer that."

"You know I'm right."

"As I was saying, you like Giorgio and Fernando for the murder."

"And/or."

"Giorgio and/or Fernando for the murder. My gut is telling me we need to look into Cyril, for several reasons."

"Like?"

"Wait. Let me finish. But we also need to look into Sue's past. Our pool of suspects may not be as small as we think. The killer could be somebody from her past."

She looked at me and grunted. "Who just happened to turn up on Halloween?"

I shrugged with my eyebrows. "Halloween may have some special significance. There may be no 'just happened' about it."

She grunted again. "What's really troubling you?"

"Cyril." We turned into Morris Park Avenue. The shops and restaurants cast amber light onto sidewalks that were turning slowly white, where the few people who were forced to brave the cold hurried toward safe, warm homes. "He behaves like a killer with a motive," I said, "but he kills like a serial killer."

FIVE

We didn't talk again until we were in the kitchen. It was too cold for beer, so we each had a tumbler of Irish whiskey. I was peeling potatoes and she was slicing eggplant and laying the slices in a colander, sprinkled with coarse salt. Then she said, quietly but suddenly:

"You've made up your mind that it's Cyril."

"I never make up my mind, Dehan, you know that. That is what evidence and proof are for. I just think he is our most likely candidate."

She raised a withering eyebrow at a slice of eggplant and dropped it in the colander. "You said, and I quote: 'He kills like a serial killer.'"

"You asked me if I have made up my mind. I haven't."

I started slicing the potatoes into nice, thick rounds and she started dicing carrots.

"All right, you want to explain to me what you mean by, 'He behaves like a killer with a motive, but he kills like a serial killer'? Or am I not smart enough to be allowed into the sanctum sanctorum of the great Sensei's mind?"

"Stop it. You are more than smart enough and you know it. I

am just not sure of my own thoughts right now. You know what the English call these?" I held up a round of potato.

She looked at it. "Potatoes?"

I shook my head. "Chips, and you have one on your shoulder. Get over it."

"Funny. Explain. And while you're explaining, get the lamb from the fridge."

I got the lamb from the fridge, then rested my ass against the side and sipped my whiskey while she put olive oil, garlic, and herbs into a big, cast-iron pan.

"Okay," I said. "The introverted, socially inadequate loner is a recurring profile among serial killers. The handing in of his notice, both at work and to his landlord, suggests careful planning, as does the killing on a notable date that is associated with death. His presence at the party is surprising, as we know that he does not like interacting with people. The same goes for his presence at the painting group. Both suggest the possibility of a predator seeking a prey."

I sipped. She fried. The smell of olive oil, thyme, and oregano was rich on the air. I inhaled, then went on.

"The killing itself bears some hallmarks of a serial killing. It is both sexual and homicidal. We know that he had a knife because he stabbed her postmortem, but there are no signs that he used the knife to terrorize her into submission. There are no cuts on her throat, and he used both hands to choke her *while* he was raping her. It is only *after* she is dead that he goes into his frenzy of stabbing. It feels methodical, almost ritualistic, like an organized serial killer getting his victim to the point where he can safely release his rage without fear of a comeback."

I sipped again.

"And finally, there is the bold, brazen leaving of his DNA and fingerprints at the scene, like a challenge to the cops: 'I can do all this and you are still not smart enough to catch me.' So much preparation, and yet no gloves and no condom. It's as though he wanted—or *needed*—to leave his mark there. It's primal, like a lion spraying to mark his territory."

I sighed. "And yet, typically, a serial killer has a territory. If he lives and works in a fixed location, he will kill nearby, within a few hours' drive, perhaps in neighboring towns.

"Alternatively, if he has a job that involves driving distances, like Adam Leroy Lane, he might kill all across the country—or the continent—like Jesperson. But what you don't get is a serial killer giving up his house and his job to move on every time he kills a victim. Either they travel or they hunt locally. They don't do both."

She shrugged and frowned, like to her it was obvious. "So our guy is not a serial killer."

"Sure, I think you're right. But, *he kills like a serial killer*. Which means his motivation is *similar* to a serial killer's."

"What does that mean?"

"I'm not sure." I walked slowly across the kitchen and leaned against the fridge, watching her as she spooned the browned meat, onions, and garlic into a deep, blue cast-iron dish, then began to lay rounds of eggplant over the top. "I'm just thinking aloud here, but a serial killer is driven by a deep, unconscious need to kill, which builds periodically and overpowers him. Usually, almost always, he is driven to kill a particular type of person. That type of person is like a symbol of what he is raging against. But what drives him is that rage, the need to kill."

"Okay."

"So, what if we have a person who has all the pain and hurt inside him that *could* lead to rage, but instead it leads him to hide away from people and become a loner, protecting himself from the hurt that people can cause him. Now let's say he meets somebody who takes a liking to him, somebody who encourages him to break out and interact with people . . ."

She froze, then turned to look at me, holding a potato round in her fingers. "Fernando."

"Cyril worked at the library. Fernando lives right next door.

He stressed that he liked him and invited him to the party. Now, I am speculating like crazy here, Dehan, but just suppose that, having allowed himself to be lured out of his safety zone, he encounters the trigger that turns his pain into rage . . ."

"Fernando telling Sue to sit on his lap and give him a kiss. He described her as a prick tease and said that that made Giorgio mad. Did she flirt with Cyril on Fernando's encouragement?"

"We don't know, but it is not a huge stretch of the imagination, and it is not beyond the bounds of possibility that if she did, that could be a trigger for his rage."

She had finished stacking the layers of meat, eggplant, and potato, and now set about making a béchamel sauce. As she did it, she nodded and said, "That is very plausible, Stone, but I am not sold. If I had come up with that, you'd have told me it was all speculation and we needed some hard evidence . . ."

"And I would have been right."

"But I am almost sold. It is a very compelling scenario. I still prefer Fernando and Giorgio, but I can see where you are coming from."

I drained my glass. "As soon as we have spoken to the witness across the road, we need to talk to Cyril's sister."

"I agree, we can call her before lunch . . ."

"No. I need to be there and look into her eyes. I need to know what kind of childhood they had together. I need to see the house where he grew up and see photographs of his mother and father. I need to be there."

She laughed as she pulled open the oven and shoved in the dish. "You just want an excuse to go to Cali and get away from the cold."

"I am outraged. Outraged, I tell you. Come here, woman. You need to be severely punished for such scandalous slander against your lord and master!"

And after that, things got complicated.

Bob Smith was in his sixties. He had a broad, Caribbean face with warm, brown eyes and tightly curled black hair that was turning gray one curl at a time. He was wearing a mulberry shirt and a sage cardigan, copper corduroy pants, and dark blue slippers. All in all, he looked comfortable. Almost as comfortable as the large, black cat he was holding in his arms, which managed to appear both expressionless and disdainful at the same time.

His voice was rich and resonant. He stood back as we showed him our badges and said, "Come on in out of the cold. It ain't a day to be outside. I have some coffee on. Have you had breakfast?"

We stepped through the white door into a small hallway where he hung up our coats. Then he led us into a warm living room with a large bow window overlooking Patterson Avenue. From that window, there was a direct view of Sue's house on the corner across the road. Dehan eyed the view and said, "We had breakfast, but we wouldn't say no to some coffee. Thanks."

He chuckled. His chuckle, like everything else about him, was comfortable. He dropped his cat on the large, cream sofa and spoke over his shoulder as he went to the kitchen.

"Make yourselves comfortable, Detectives. I won't be but two minutes."

Dehan went over to the window and I sat in one of his large, cream calico chairs. A *New York Times* lay in pieces on the sofa, and the cat was in the process of turning it into a shredded nest. On the heavy, oak coffee table there was a copy of *Catch-22*. By the look of it, he had read it several times.

After five minutes, Bob Smith returned with a tray bearing a coffeepot, three cups and saucers, a dish of brownies, sugar, milk, and cream. He set it on the table, sat himself on the sofa, and smiled. He did both things comfortably.

"It *was* twelve years ago last Halloween," he said as he poured a black stream of brew into a cup and handed it to Dehan. "Please help yourself to sugar and cream, and a cookie." He picked up another cup and poured. "But when you telephoned this morning, I sat and thought about it, and I am pretty sure my memory is accurate."

He handed me a cup, and I sat back while he poured his own and kept talking.

"I am an amateur mathematician," he said. "After I studied mathematics part time at NYU." He sat back and sipped. "I am not a mathematical genius or anything like that. Just an aficionado, but I have always liked to keep my mind agile and strong: attention, concentration, observation. I am very observant, and I retain what I observe."

I smiled. "Admirable. So what did you observe that night, Mr. Smith?"

He pointed at his windowsill. "I had a pumpkin in the window, to signal to the children of the neighborhood that they could come and trick or treat at my door. I usually keep the drapes open on Halloween until about one a.m., as a lot of the children around here stay up late that night.

"However, that particular night I had been reading, and I had dozed off. I was awakened at about two twenty by a woman shouting. I went to look and saw my then neighbor, Sue, with a young man. They were at the top of her stairs—you see that she has a steep flight of thirteen steps leading up to her door on the second floor—he was speaking quietly. She seemed to be a little inebriated and kept shouting, 'No means no!' and knocking his hands away as he tried to take her shoulders . . ."

Dehan frowned and pointed at the window. "You could hear her? Only I see you have triple glazing."

He nodded. "Oh, yes. When I saw what was happening, I opened the window, intending to call to her and ask if she was all right. But then, when I saw that he wasn't taking no for an answer, I went to get my telephone. It is wireless, but I don't use a cell anymore. One of the pleasures of retirement." He smiled, comfortably. "When I got back, the man had descended the stairs and was walking away. She was gone and her door was closed."

I leaned forward. "The door was definitely closed?"

"Oh yes, definitely." He gave a smile that suggested the answer was obvious. "Had she left it open, I would have called her. However, just as I was pulling the drapes closed, another man approached from the direction of the party. He climbed the stairs and rang her bell. After a moment, the door opened, they seemed to exchange some words, not in an unfriendly way, he stepped in, and the door closed behind him. I assumed all was well, closed my drapes, and went to bed."

Dehan nodded for a moment, sipping her coffee. Then she asked, "Could you describe the two men? Did you know either of them?"

He sighed and stroked his cat. "Please, let me give you a cautious answer. I should hate for an innocent man to go to prison because of my erroneous identification. That said, I had the impression at the time that the first man was a friend of Giorgio, the Mexican artist who lives up the road, where the party was being held that night. I don't know his name, but I have seen them together on many occasions. Average height, slim, well-built, curly hair. He looks something like Carlos Santana, if that name means anything to you. The second man was not dissimilar, but it was much harder to make any kind of identification because he was so wrapped up with clothes, including a thick woolen hat."

Dehan scratched her chin. "I don't want to influence you, Mr. Smith..."

"You won't, don't worry."

"Good. Is it possible that the second man *was* the first man, having returned after putting on warmer clothes?"

His eyebrows shot up. "Well, now, that is something that had never occurred to me. Yes, it is certainly *possible*, but I could not put my hand on my heart and say it certainly was him. Also, I would have to say I doubt it, because she was so adamant in rejecting the first man that I think it unlikely."

"But you would say he was roughly the same height and size."

"Yes."

I drained my cup and set it down on the table. "When he rang on the bell, and the door opened, did you see Sue?"

He looked surprised again and chuckled. "My, you two have an interesting line in questions." He leaned back against the sofa and thought for a moment. "One is so cautious about creating false memories. Did I see her, or just assume that I had seen her? No, I saw her. She pulled the door open, she had taken off her coat, they spoke a moment, she was smiling, and they went inside. She closed the door."

"I am sure your recollection is very accurate, Mr. Smith, but can I just make sure? Are you absolutely certain that the first man left?"

"Oh, without a doubt. I returned with the telephone, and the very reason I did not call 911 was because he was leaving."

"Yes, that makes perfect sense. Did you hear any of the exchange between the second man and Sue?"

"No. I had by then closed the window."

Dehan crossed one long leg over the other. "How well did you know Sue?"

He smiled with pleasure. "Not all that well, sadly. Not as well as I should have liked." He laughed. "She was immensely attractive. I don't just mean her looks, but her temperament, her personality. She was very lively and very friendly. Always smiling. So if she passed and I was doing some gardening she would stop and we would chat. She was quite bright. She had an opinion on most things. She liked to go to exhibitions. Her interest in art was genuine. But we had not become that friendly that we would visit with each other or anything of that sort."

She winced at her own question. "Would you say she was a flirt?"

He produced his comfortable chuckle again and nodded. "Oh, yes. She was definitely a flirt. But not in a malicious way. I think a lot of younger men would have mistaken her flirting for a come-on. She was not skilled, but she loved the game. In my youth, these things were better understood, but today, sadly, I see a youth that wants immediate gratification for every whim and desire, and also a youth that is deeply confused about its own identity. She loved the whole game of flirting, but I was aware that she had not yet found a man that she wanted a serious relationship with." He shrugged with his eyebrows and sadness altered his features. "Perhaps she flirted with the wrong man."

I grunted. "Did she have many male visitors?"

He watched me awhile with a glimmer of amusement in his eyes. "I liked her, Detective Stone, I was fond of her, but I didn't spend my life watching her through my window. I have children and grandchildren, and a girlfriend to keep me busy."

"None of that surprises me, Mr. Smith."

"I just wanted to make sure you understood that. The answer to your question is that the only men I saw visiting her were the Mexican artist and his friend, sometimes together and sometimes separately. How long they stayed I have no idea, and as to whether there were others, there may well have been. But those two were the only ones I saw."

We were silent for a moment, then I asked him, "Did you form any private opinion or theory about who might have killed her?"

He shook his head. "No, I simply didn't know her well enough."

We chatted a little longer, then thanked him for his help and left, no wiser than we had been when we'd arrived.

SIX

There were patches of ice blue in the sky. The sleet had stopped, leaving the pavements wet and slippery, but the temperature had dropped to several degrees below freezing, causing patches of black ice to form on the roads. A cruel wind was gusting in off the East River, and the last few dead leaves that had been clinging on, like rotten teeth in an old man's head, were finally letting go of their branches and falling to be crushed and trodden into sludge. Soon it would snow heavily. You could feel it in the air.

As we drove slowly back through the damp cold toward the 43rd, I played an old Mamas and the Papas song in my head and wondered about Cyril's sister in California.

"I'm going to talk to the inspector," I said. "We need to know about Cyril's background. I also find it hard to believe that his sister doesn't know where he is."

"Good," she said from under her shapeless woolen hat. "While you do that, I'm going to call the library, and also track down Cyril's landlord. Maybe we can have a chat with him before we go to Cali." She glanced at me and shrugged. "To be honest, we're clutching at straws, Stone. I don't hold out much hope for this case. I think this is the one that got away. But you never know, right? When he gave notice, he might have said something about where he was going." She sighed. "We also need to know more about Sue's past. If I have time, I'll get started on that too."

I parked and we made our way unsteadily across the icy road to the entrance. There, Dehan went into the detectives' room, and I climbed the stairs to Deputy Inspector John Newman's office. I knocked and went in. He was standing, watering a bonsai fig tree on his windowsill. Outside, the sunlight had faded on Story Avenue, leaving a gray translucence in its place.

"Good morning, John," he said, and smiled without looking at me. "What can I do for you?"

I closed the door. "We're looking into the Sue Benedict case, sir."

He frowned and shook his head at the diminutive fig tree, like it was a naughty fig tree. "Nope," he said.

"It's twelve years old. Young woman found raped and murdered in her apartment on Patterson Avenue. They got a perfect DNA profile and a perfect set of finger and thumbprints from her throat, but there was no match on CODIS, IAFIS, or among the people who'd attended the Halloween party she was at."

He made a small "harrumph" noise, gestured to a chair, and returned to his own behind the desk. "A case worthy of your and Dehan's talents," he said, and smiled in the same comfortable way Bob Smith had. "How do you plan to tackle it?"

"There was just one guest, sir, who was not tested. Cyril Browne. He was a member of the same art class she went to, and he was also at the Halloween party that night. However, next morning he had vanished without a trace. The curious thing was that he had given both his landlord and his job notice that he was quitting, two months earlier."

The inspector frowned and picked up a pencil, wagging it by the eraser as he narrowed his eyes. "He had planned to kill her for two months, then he struck after the Halloween party?"

"It's possible. We are trying to track him down. His only

known relative is his sister, but she lives outside Sacramento, in California."

He raised an eyebrow at me. "How do you manage it, Stone? Every winter you come up with a case that requires a trip to California."

I spoke without expression. "It was Dehan who chose the case, sir."

He chuckled, and for a moment I wondered if he was related to Bob Smith. It was the same comfortable chuckle. "Can this woman not be contacted on the telephone?"

"Back in the day, Detective Rafa Montilla did just that. I believe his investigation was pretty exhaustive. However, she stonewalled him, and my gut is telling me that she has at least some idea of where Cyril is." Before he could challenge me on the accuracy of my gut, I moved swiftly on. "In fact, sir, I am pretty certain that his family plays an important part in this case. From what we have been able to ascertain from other witnesses, he seems to have been a rather . . ." I hesitated. "A rather *troubled* young man: extremely withdrawn, introverted, and, according to one of the witnesses, possibly obsessed with the victim. I think it's important that we get some insight into his background, to help understand him and track him down, and for that I think we need to confront his sister in person."

He nodded. "You know I trust your judgment, John. Just don't turn it into a holiday. I know you won't. What else are you doing, back here?"

"Reinterviewing the witnesses, having a second look at the DNA and fingerprints, running them through the databases again in case he has offended since and been caught. And we are going to talk to his ex-employer and his landlord, see if they know anything."

He pursed his lips in a way that said he approved, and gave a single nod. "Good, keep me posted on any developments. Let me know when you're heading off for Sacramento. You'll fly, I take it."

I told him we would and trotted back down the stairs to find Dehan clutching a large paper cup of coffee and staring at her laptop. I dropped into my chair, stretched out my legs, and laced my fingers over my belly. "You keep drinking so much coffee your hair will go frizzy and your eyes will start bulging."

Mo, at the desk across the aisle, looked over and nodded. "It's true, that happened to a friend of my cousin in Detroit."

We both narrowed our eyes at him.

He shrugged and went back to his work. "Whatever."

Dehan said, "I called the library and spoke to the current manager. She vaguely remembered Cyril. She said he was a pain in the ass and never spoke to anybody. He certainly gave no indication of where he was going, and nobody cared anyway. They were just glad to see him leave. The manager at the time died five years ago, so I couldn't speak to him. So that was pretty much a dead end."

"Okay, how about his landlord?"

"Amir Javid. He now occupies the house Cyril had back then, corner of Thieriot and O'Brien. Apparently he has several properties he lets out, but this is the nicest, so he lives there now. He's a chatty guy. He remembers Cyril because of the murder, and he is happy to see us in the next half hour, if that suits us. How did you get on?"

I smiled over at Mo and raised my voice slightly. "The chief gave us the go-ahead to fly to California as soon as we're done with Javid."

Mo turned a baleful stare on me.

I kept smiling at him and talking to Dehan. "He said he agrees with me that it is essential to the investigation that we fly to California as soon as possible, and take as long as we need there."

Dehan snorted and Mo shook his head. "You, you two, you just . . . you're so . . . *yah*!" He flapped his hand at me and turned back again to whatever it was he was doing.

Dehan stood and pulled on her coat, grinning. "What you

working on, Mo? Something interesting? That mugging on Lafayette?"

"Go to hell!"

"First California," I said, "then hell."

We left behind us an unsympathetic silence.

Cyril had lived just one block from Sue's apartment. It was the last house before the park, on the corner of Thieriot and O'Brien Avenue. Beyond the park was the river, and there was a freezing, blustery wind coming off the water when we arrived. The house was set back from the road among well-kept lawns, behind a very elaborate, green wrought iron fence. The first thing I saw as I entered the drive was the garage, then a small path that led off to the side and took me to the front of the house. Javid saw us approaching through the living room window, waved, and hurried to let us in.

"Please," was his first word, as he opened the door and gestured us toward the living room, where a log fire was burning in the hearth. "Please," he said again. "Make yourselves comfortable. My wife is making coffee. It is a most inhospitable day. Can I offer you anything else? Something to eat, perhaps?"

We showed him our badges, confirmed who we were, and I added, "Please don't trouble your wife, Mr. Javid. We won't take up much of your time."

We sat in front of the fire, each of us perched on the edge of our chairs, as though we were all trying to get closer to the heat of the flames.

He said, "You want to know about Cyril Browne? There is not much I can tell you. He was a very private man. Always paid very punctually. No problems there at all. He gave me notice that he was leaving in two months, as per our contract . . ."

Dehan cut in. "Did he give you any idea why he was leaving, or where he was going?"

He became abstracted, winced slightly at the memory. "He didn't speak very clearly. No, that isn't true." He tilted his head and wagged his finger in the negative. "That isn't true. He spoke clearly enough, all right, but very *quietly*. So it was very difficult to catch the things that he said. And his face was always averted, as though he were ashamed or embarrassed by eye contact. But, once I thought he said that he was going home. It was jumbled in with a lot of other stuff that he was saying, but I got that impression. 'Time to go home,' or 'Time to come home.' Something like that. But why he was leaving? He never said anything about that. Unless"—he shrugged—"it was because it was time to go home!"

It didn't make a lot of sense to me, so I asked, "How well did you know him, Mr. Javid? Did he ever talk to you about back home, about his family?"

Javid shook his head and smiled. "No, no, never anything like that."

"Was there anything he said, any passing comments that might give us a clue as to the nature of the man, what made him tick, interests, anything . . . ?"

He shook his head again. "No, no, as I say, he spoke little, and what he said was very quiet. He certainly never invited intimacy, friendship, or conversation."

He paused, and Dehan gave me a look that was eloquent of despair. We were up against a brick wall, and I could sense her thinking this was going to be the case we couldn't crack. But I could also see Javid frowning, hesitating. I said, "What is it, Mr. Javid? However insignificant it may seem, it might turn out to be helpful."

"Well, there was one thing . . ." A look of severity came over his face and his lips stretched into a tight, thin line. "It is a little embarrassing, but, after he had gone, while I was cleaning up and making the place ready for the next tenants, I found, tucked down the side of the cushion on his preferred armchair, a card."

I frowned. "What kind of card?"

"A *business* card, belonging to a woman. Her name was Xara, with an *X*, X-A-R-A, and she offered services that were very explicitly sexual. I do not know why America permits this kind of thing. Imagine if a family with children had taken the house and found that card! It is very immoral and offensive to God."

I looked at Dehan, and she was frowning back at me. I said, "Mr. Javid, this could be extremely important. Do you happen to remember anything else, at all, about this card? The number, perhaps . . . ?"

He straightened his back and dignity stiffened his neck and made him raise his nose and chin in the air. I thought he was going to tell us he threw the card straight in the trash, but instead he said, "In fact, as it happens, I made a note of the details in my address book, because I thought maybe one day the police might be interested."

"That was very perceptive of you, Mr. Javid." I tried to keep the irony from my voice and avoided Dehan's eye. He stood and went out to the hall. There he pulled a slim, black diary from his coat pocket and returned to sit down.

"She goes by the name Xara Xubmissive. Her telephone number was . . ." He recited the number and added, "I have never called her, obviously, and this was twelve years ago, so I don't know if she will still be in New York or if she will be of any help to you. This kind of people are often liars and very duplicitous, as I am sure you know from your work, but I am quite sure he used to visit her."

Dehan smiled blandly and blinked. "There isn't much we haven't come across in our work, Mr. Javid, and we certainly know how to spot a duplicitous lie, believe me."

He looked uncomfortable and turned to me. "That really is all I can tell you about him. I suppose the most notable thing about Cyril was that there was absolutely nothing notable about him. Apart, of course, from his apparent penchant for naughty women."

We thanked him, shook hands, and stepped out into the icy wind again. We stood at the car a moment, Dehan gazing out at the inky, choppy waters of the river, I gazing up along Thieriot Avenue, toward the corner with Patterson. "What is that?" I said.

"Three hundred yards? Two strides per second, a hundred and fifty seconds, two and a half minutes . . ."

Dehan nodded and pointed out at the dark water. "And that right there is where the knife and his bloodstained clothes are." She turned to look at me. "Let's go talk to the submissive Xara before we go to California."

I sighed. "For sure. Rogers works Vice. Why don't you give him a call? He might know her."

We climbed in the car, and as I pulled away, she was dialing. After a moment, she asked to be put through to Detective Rogers, in Vice, then said:

"Rogers, hey, it's Dehan . . . Yeah, not bad. He's good too. Listen, we're looking for a hooker . . ." She paused, watching the road go by. "Uh-huh, that's funny. I never heard that one before . . ." She looked at me, rolled her eyes, and shook her head. "No, yeah, things are great with us, don't worry about it. He told me he wanted me to moan more. I told him, 'Such a day I had! I never stop working. The car broke down. Now I have no car . . .' but apparently that's not what he meant. Yeah, I thought you'd like that one. Now listen to me, will you? Her name is Xara Xubmissive, both with an *X* instead of an *S*, apparently she's submissive. Subtle, right? . . . Yeah? You know her? No, not in the biblical sense. Right, give me her number and address, will you?" She took out her pen, grabbed my left hand, and jotted down the number and the address on my palm. "Yeah, thanks, Rogers, you're a real asshole. Take it easy." She hung up and said again, "Asshole. Thirteen oh nine B, Seneca Avenue. The number has changed." She grinned. "So Javid hasn't called in a while."

SEVEN

Thirteen oh nine Seneca Avenue was across the river in Hunts Point. It was a redbrick box with an arched porch and a dead tree in the front yard. We rang and hammered for five minutes until we heard the slip and flap of slippers approaching the door. It was yanked open and a large peroxide blonde in her early fifties stood squinting at us through two coils of smoke that were issuing slowly from her nostrils. She was wearing a large pink bathrobe and pink fluffy slippers. Between her bathrobe and the slippers she had plump white legs that needed shaving. She said:

"You look like cops."

Dehan was smiling and breathing condensation into her palms. She pulled out her badge and showed it. "I'm Detective Dehan, this is my partner, Detective Stone. Are you Xara, with an *X*?"

"Yeah, I'm Xara with an *X*, *X* for sex, *X* marks the spot. What do you want?"

"We just want to ask you some questions about Cyril Browne."

She screwed up her face like she'd bitten into a lemon. "*Who?* Are you Vice? Why ain't Rogers with you?"

"Can we come in, Xara? It's kind of cold out here."

She sighed a big, noisy sigh, turned, and walked away, leaving the door open. I said, "I think that means we can go in. After you, Detective Dehan with an *H*."

We followed her down a dark green, threadbare carpet to a small kitchen at the back of the house. There was a vinyl floor, a sink stacked with dirty dishes, a fold-down table made of steel tubing and Formica, and two chairs of the same design. She sat on one of them, beside a mug of coffee, an overfilled ashtray, and a cell phone.

"I was working," she said, as though in answer to an unspoken question. "'Swhy I couldn't open the door. They pay before they get put through, so you gotta finish the session, or they don't call back. You can't leave the guy halfway, right?"

I rested my ass against the draining board and Dehan leaned on the doorjamb. We watched her crush out a cigarette and pull another from a carton. She spoke without looking up, with the cigarette between her lips as she lit it with a green disposable lighter.

"What d'you say his name was?"

Dehan said, "Cyril Browne."

She shrugged her plump shoulders and coughed smoke. "That name don't mean nothin' to me."

"This is going back twelve years."

"*Twelve years?* Are you kidding me? Do you know how many men I seen in the last twelve years? True, in the last couple a years I work mainly on the telephone, but honey, do the math. Five Johns a day, five days a week, for ten years? What is that?"

I smiled. "That's thirteen thousand Johns, Xara."

She stared at me a moment. "Thirteen *thousand*? Seriously?"

"Seriously. I guess some are repeat customers, right? They get to know you, they like your engaging personality and they come back."

She smiled. It wasn't a pretty sight. "You're sweet."

Dehan said, "Cyril was a bit odd."

"All my clients are a bit odd, baby. That's why they're my clients."

"He lived in Soundview, worked at the library, painfully shy . . ."

Xara sucked on her cigarette, looked over at the plates stacked in the sink.

Dehan went on, "Very quiet spoken, not bad looking, learning to paint . . ." She pulled out her phone, flipped the screen a couple of times, and showed Xara a picture.

Xara glanced at it and spoke to the washing up. "You ain't Vice, you's Homicide."

I said, "No, we're a cold-case unit. What do you know about Cyril?"

"I remember him 'cause of the girl. 'Cause of the murder. He disappeared, and all of a sudden they was lookin' for him." She shook her head. "I couldn't believe . . ." She stopped talking and looked down at her cigarette. Her expression was one almost of anger. "I don't believe he killed nobody."

"How well did you know him?"

She shrugged, still examining the burning tip of her cigarette. "I guess I knew him pretty good. Better than most people. We was close in the end." We waited in silence. A gust of wind rattled the glass in the kitchen window. She flicked ash. "He used to come once a week. Always on a Sunday. Sometimes he'd come twice if he was feelin' bad. I liked him." She drew smoke deep into her lungs and spoke as it trailed out among her lipstick and her words. "You never have feeling for your clients. You can't do that in this business. Specially . . ." She looked up at us, first at me and then at Dehan. "Specially if you advertise as sub. You know what that means? It means submissive. If you're submissive, they treat you like trash. It's what they're payin' you for. So you ain't never gonna meet a client you like. It stands to reason. But Cyril . . ." She smiled. "Poor schmuck. What kind a mom calls her boy Cyril? You might as well cut off his balls at birth. That boy is gonna suffer all his life. Cyril was lookin' for a sub, not so he could treat her like trash, but just so she'd be nice to him! And kind, and tender. He didn't want to dominate nobody. He didn't want to hurt nobody. He just wanted somebody who would not hurt him."

Dehan took the chair across from Xara. She was frowning. "How long was he coming here, Xara?"

"Shit, I don't know. Few months. Regular like clockwork. He used to call them his session . . ." She laughed, and there was genuine fondness in her face. "Like I was some kind a fancy shrink. He talked a lot about his work. He hated the people he worked with. Said they hated him too."

I said, "Did he ever mention his classmates, where he was learning to paint?"

She nodded, gazing out of the window at the leaden, cold sky and the naked trees in the backyard. "Yeah, he did. It's twelve years ago, so if I get the details wrong don't give me a hard time. I'm just tellin' you how I remember it. He said they was all fancy-pants arty types. His teacher was a prick. Some Mexican asshole, no offense to the Mexicans. Some of my best friends is Mexican whores, know what I'm sayin'? But this particular Mexican was an asshole, according to Cyril. Really thought he was somethin' special. An' then there was the girl who got killed . . ."

"Sue?"

"I don't remember her name. It might have been Sue. He said she was nice, and he'd like her to notice him from time to time, but she only had eyes for the Mexican prick. And then . . ."

She stopped talking, flicked ash from her cigarette, and picked up her mug. She swirled the contents around and watched it for a moment. Then drank.

"This makes me sad, remembering this," she said at last. "There was another guy. These are the ones I remember because he talked about them the most. Did the Mexican guy have a brother? He said this guy was nice to him sometimes, laughed at him, but tried to help him get closer to Sue, encouraged him to be a bit bolder with women. It was this guy's idea he should come and see me, a whore, a submissive whore. Tried to bring him out of himself, know what I mean?"

"Did this guy ever come and see you?"

She shook her head. "Not that I'm aware of, but I don't ask them for their fuckin' résumés, right?" She sniffed, then carried on. "He showed me some of his paintings. Gave me a couple. I got them upstairs. They was nice. Did one of me, a portrait. It was good."

She fell silent. I watched her a moment and scratched my Adam's apple. "Xara, if he wasn't looking for sub-dom sex, what was he looking for? Sexually, I mean. Was he ever violent to you? Did he ever become angry or aggressive?"

She looked surprised and stared at me a moment. "No, never. He wasn't lookin' for any kind of sex. We tried a few times, but he couldn't get it up. Honey, I tried everything in the book and a few things that was never writ down in the book. He just couldn't get past Mr. Floppy."

Dehan flopped back in her chair.

Xara turned to look at her. "I ain't kidding. That's why I don't believe he could'a done that murder. He could no more rape a woman than I could. And I ain't got a dick."

I squinted at her. "What about Viagra, Cialis..."

"Forget it! Ain't I tellin' you we tried everything? He wasn't even interested. All he wanted was a woman to be sweet to him: hug him, hold him, stroke his hair, say sweet things to him. He *loved* bein' told he was handsome. Truth is he wasn't bad lookin'. Nice face. But his dick was like last night's fuckin' Chinese noodles. As limp as a boiled shrimp."

Dehan was staring at the wall. "I'll be damned!"

Xara looked at her and laughed. "Ain't nobody in this room goin' to the Good Place, that's for sure!"

I raised an eyebrow at her and smiled. "So he gave you no indication that he was planning to leave?"

"Uh-uh. He just stopped calling and stopped showin' up."

"Okay, now think about this very carefully before you answer,

Xara. Was there anything he said to you, any passing comment, anything at all that would give you some clue to where he might have gone?"

She held my eye for a long moment. Her expression was not friendly. "I already told you, I liked the boy. You get your filthy hands on him, and you gonna frame him for a murder he did not commit. So even if I had some idea, which I ain't, I wouldn't tell the likes of you, Mr. Gammon."

Dehan sighed. "We don't want to frame him, Xara. We just want to know what happened that night. If he didn't kill Sue, we need to eliminate him as a suspect. Because right now there is a man out there who *did* kill Sue, who may have killed again—who may still be killing. We want to stop this killer, whoever he is. We're not in the business of framing anybody."

She made a face that was skeptical. "Tell that to your buddies in Vice." She shook her head. "I don't know. He talked a lot about going home. Only he didn't say it like that. He used to say 'comin' home,' 'I wanna come home,' he'd say, like that had some special meaning for him. I know he was from Sacramento. I don't know if he was thinkin' of going back to California. I know he liked the desert, but I don't think he was happy out west. He never talked about his family. He said once he had a sister, but he never talked about her." She crushed out the butt in the ashtray and fiddled with the packet, turning it around in her plump, white fingers. "I know what that's like, not wanting to talk about your family." She snorted. "Whatever he thought, I ain't no shrink, but I know he weren't happy as a kid. You could see that plain as day." She hesitated. "And you know what else you could see?"

I jerked my chin at her in a wordless "What?"

"He wouldn't hurt a fly. He come across as sullen and rude sometimes, but it was *de*fensive, not *o*ffensive. That was his way of protecting himself. Underneath that shell, he was the softest, sweetest boy I ever met."

I looked at Dehan. She shrugged. I said, "Okay, Xara. Thanks for your time. You've been very helpful."

She laughed a smoky laugh and started coughing. "I been helpful to the cops. I'm goin' to whore hell for sure."

We let ourselves out. As I closed the door, I could still hear her coughing in the kitchen. The sudden cold air made us shiver, and I thrust my hands deep in my pockets.

Dehan said, "The softest, sweetest boy a submissive hooker ever met isn't much of a recommendation."

I grunted. "But it was a very believable picture. What time is it?"

"Eleven. Too early for lunch, Stone."

"Let's grab a coffee and a snack somewhere. This is one hell of a puzzle, Dehan. I need to think this through."

We went to Monsignor Raul Del Valle Square and hustled inside the Café Sevilla. It was warm and close, it smelled of wet coats and sweet buns, and there was an espresso machine screaming behind the bar. We found a table by the window, squeezed in, and ordered two cups of hot chocolate and two almond paste croissants. Then we sat and stared out at the soaking sludge and the traffic in silence. Dehan was the first to speak after the waitress had brought our order. She broke off a piece of croissant and dunked it in her chocolate.

"She just blew a hole a mile wide in our case, Stone."

I smiled at her. "In my case. Your money was on Fernando and Giorgio."

She tilted her head in a kind of one-shouldered shrug. "You had me almost sold on your semi–serial killer theory, but I have to admit—the sweetest guy she ever met, who wouldn't hurt a fly, *and* he has erectile dysfunction not even Viagra can cure . . . that's not much of a prime suspect."

I nodded. "You're right. But I still think we need to track him down and talk to him. He is still the one guy who didn't give a sample, and he is the one guy who disappeared the very next morning after the killing. It's too much of a coincidence."

She frowned at her croissant and made a "hm" sound, then said, "I agree, but Stone, maybe we need to look at this again. Like

I said before, maybe we've been making assumptions." She leaned forward and put both elbows on the table. "Okay, so two months earlier, late August, he hands in his notice at work and to his landlord, and because of that we have assumed that this meant he intended to vanish. But actually, when you think about it, it does not, in itself, mean he was planning to disappear from New York at all. He might have been moving next door. He might have been offered a better job and was planning to move up the road, or to Brooklyn."

"Okay..."

"So his notice could well be totally unrelated to his disappearance."

"What are you driving at?"

She took a bite of her croissant and sat chewing for a moment. "Suppose Giorgio and Fernando have been trying to get into Sue's pants for some time, they both implied as much, but Sue, despite being a flirt, is, as her neighbor Bob Smith said, at heart a good, decent girl next door. We only have Giorgio and Fernando's word for it that she was a tease, and for how she was behaving at the party."

"True."

"So let's imagine for a moment a different scenario. Fernando has been encouraging Sue and Cyril to talk to each other, telling her to sit on his lap, yadda yadda. He's doing this because he thinks it's funny, he's getting a laugh out of Cyril: the more Cyril humiliates himself, the better Fernando looks and feels. But, to his surprise, it has the opposite effect of what he expects. Why? Because Sue is, in fact, like Bob said, a nice person. And so is Cyril, and when they are pushed together, they actually start to like each other and become friends. Plus, Fernando and Giorgio are getting on her nerves and Cyril is actually nice to her." She paused. "I know it's a lot of speculation, but stay with me, 'cause it's all we have right now. So, at two o'clock that morning, Sue is a bit drunk, but really, basically, she's had enough of Giorgio and Fernando coming on to her and she just wants to go home. So she leaves. Fernando goes after her, determined he is going to sleep with her that night. She tells him to take a hike. No means no. Okay so far?"

"Yeah, as you say, a lot of speculation, but it's making sense."

"So she goes home to her apartment. With Sue gone, Cyril has no reason to stay at the party. So he leaves too, but on the way home he passes by her place to check she's okay. Meanwhile, Fernando has gone back to Giorgio to report on his failure. They are both drunk, maybe stoned, and they decide they have had enough of Sue and what they see as her 'prick teasing.' Remember, they *both* described her in so many words as a prick tease. Tonight they are going to have her whether she likes it or not."

"Hmm . . . It's feasible."

"Shut up. Listen. When they get there, they find that not only has she rejected them but, to add insult to injury, she is with the nerd. This is too much for their narcissistic egos, they get real mad, and they kill her. Cyril freaks, panics, and runs. Nothing to do with handing in his notice."

"It's good, but it has a major flaw, Dehan."

"I know, the semen. The DNA. But there might be an explanation for that."

"I think I know . . ."

"Shut up, listen, give me my moment. If his erectile dysfunction was emotional—not a physical condition—and Xara was actually having a therapeutic effect on him, like he said, Sue might actually have aroused him. If he was in love with her, and she was sweet and nice to him, maybe they actually got it on. It wasn't rape at all."

"Wow, that is one hell of a theory, Dehan."

She nodded, using her whole body, and stuffed the last of her almond croissant in her mouth. "I rike idge. I' burksh fo me."

"You like it and it works for you."

"Mm-hm."

I thought about it, turned it over in my mind, looking at the angles. Finally I said, "Well, if we are going to prove it, we need

Cyril Browne more than ever. Let's go report to the chief and book them tickets. I also want him to run a check on Giorgio and Fernando, see if they have any priors out of state."

"No road trip?" she said, licking her fingers and draining her cup.

"Not this time, Ritoo Glasshopper. This time we fly."

EIGHT

WE TOUCHED DOWN AT SACRAMENTO MATHER AIRPORT at ten past ten that night. It was cold as we stepped out into the parking lot, but it wasn't freezing, and it wasn't sleeting. That was a relief. From there it was a twenty-minute drive, in an Avis hire car, west along the Lincoln Highway and then south on Watt Avenue, to Elk Grove, where Dehan had booked us into the Holiday Inn on Laguna Boulevard. By the time we had unpacked and hung up our clothes, it was eleven p.m., two in the morning in New York. We were spent, so we had a drink from the minibar and hit the sack.

Next morning at eight we had a soulless breakfast of bagels and coffee in a soulless breakfast room; but after that we stepped out into bright sunshine, climbed in the car, and rolled down the windows for a pleasant two-mile drive to Cyril's sister's house, on Kilconnell Drive. According to the file, her name was Mary Browne, and she lived on her own opposite the elementary school where she taught. We hadn't called to let her know we were coming because we wanted to surprise her.

Kilconnell Drive is a very pleasant road, with attractive houses, broad, green lawns, and an abundance of trees. We pulled up outside Mary Browne's house and I checked my watch. It was ten minutes before nine. I looked at Dehan. She grimaced. "Let's see if she sends us back to New York."

I opened the door. "That ain't gonna happen."

She followed me up the drive, past the garage, and up to the front door, in the shade of a large green oak. I rang the bell, and a few moments later the door was opened by an oddly familiar woman. She was big, with blond hair, a tweed skirt, and sensible shoes. She had on a very white blouse and a string of pearls around her neck. Her face was soft and round, but her expression was hard and sharp. I guessed she was in her late fifties but might have been older. She said:

"Well?"

"Good morning." I didn't bother to smile. "We are detectives from the New York Police Department. This is Detective Carmen Dehan, and I am Detective John Stone." We showed her our badges, but she didn't look at them. Her face had gone hard. I ignored her expression and went on. "We have notified the Elk Grove PD that we are here, ma'am. We are conducting some inquiries related to an investigation back in New York. Would you mind answering a few questions for us?"

"What about? I can't imagine that I would have any information of interest to the New York Police Department."

"Are you Mary Browne?"

"Of course I am!"

"Ms. Browne, we would like to ask you about your brother, Cyril. Could we possibly come inside?"

"Could you not have telephoned? Do you not have telephones in New York?"

I smiled a bland kind of smile. "Ms. Browne, we have traveled two and a half thousand miles to ask you a couple of questions. We won't take up much of your time, but we would be very grateful if you would let us in."

"I have nothing to say."

"If this is not a convenient time, we can come back . . ."

"I have told you, I have nothing to say."

I sighed. She reached for the door to slam it in my face. I spoke quietly. "We will come back with the Elk Grove PD, ma'am, in cars, with sirens, with a search warrant, and we will take you in cuffs to the station for questioning."

Her face went like chalk and her mouth sagged. "You can't do that! On what grounds?"

"Obstruction of justice is the least of the charges I will bring against you. Aiding and abetting a murder suspect, harboring a suspected criminal . . . That's just for starters. Now, Ms. Browne, why don't you do yourself a favor, let us in and just answer a few, simple questions."

She stood back and held the door.

We went through to a large, open-plan room with a mezzanine floor. One wall was taken up with sliding glass doors that led onto a patio and a back lawn. The floors were polished hardwood with rugs, and the chairs and the sofa were in dark leather. There was a cold, empty fireplace. Two small steps led to the higher level, where there was a dining table. I looked for family photographs. There were none.

On the sofa, I noticed an embroidery basket and a hoop. Held in the hoop was a piece of white linen with an attractive and intricate peacock embroidered on it. The work was almost finished but for a few tail feathers. Pierced into the cloth, as though she had been embroidering when we called, was a small needle with a trailing red thread, knotted at the end.

I sat in an armchair without being asked. Mary's face said she didn't like that, but I didn't care, and my face said that. She sat at the far end of the sofa, and Dehan took the other chair. I said:

"Ms. Browne, I think I had better explain the situation to you. It is important that you understand exactly what is going on here. Your brother was a suspect in the murder of Sue Benedict, twelve years ago. DNA and fingerprints were found on the victim, but no match was found in the police databases. Everybody who was at the Halloween party Sue had attended just before she was killed gave samples of DNA and their prints. None of them matched.

The only person who was at the party and did not provide a sample was Cyril. Because he had vanished."

I waited a moment to see if she would say anything. She remained immobile and silent, with her hands clasped in her lap.

"These circumstances naturally made him a suspect. However, in the last couple of days, since my partner and I have taken this case, we have come across evidence that suggests very strongly that he did not kill Sue Benedict."

A cautious frown creased her brow. "What kind of evidence?"

I drew breath, but it was Dehan who answered. "Sue was raped by whoever killed her. Your brother had severe erectile dysfunction. He couldn't achieve an erection even with the help of Viagra. Therefore he could not have raped her, even if he'd wanted to."

Her expression said it was the first time in her life she had ever heard the word "erection" spoke aloud. Then, as the implications of what she had been told began to sink in, her expression changed. Her eyes jerked this way and that, with little twitches of her eyebrows. I gave her a moment to assimilate the importance of what Dehan had said.

"It is still extremely important that we talk to Cyril. Apart from the killer, he may be the last person to have seen Sue Benedict alive. We believe he may well have seen the killer. Besides which, Ms. Browne, if he is innocent he needs to be cleared. He must be living in hell right now."

She raised her eyes to meet mine. "I actually have no idea where he is, Detective Stone."

I shook my head. "I don't believe you."

"I can't help that." She straightened her tweed skirt over her knees. The room was very quiet. Somewhere I could hear the tick of an old-fashioned clock. It made the house seem quieter.

"Cyril and I were very close as children. But after he went to New York, we lost touch. I always tried to look out for him, but it seems he didn't appreciate that. We didn't communicate for quite a few years. Not even Christmas cards."

She looked up, raised her chin, as though challenging me to make something of the fact that they hadn't exchanged Christmas cards. When I said nothing, she looked back at the hem of her skirt.

"Then, quite suddenly, twelve years ago, out of the blue, he telephoned me. He said he was in serious trouble and needed my help, just for a few days."

Dehan asked her, "What kind of help?"

Mary closed her eyes. She made an eloquent expression of impatience. "It was absolute nonsense. Typical of Cyril's. Melodramatic nonsense. He said he was in trouble with the police. He had been framed for *murder*, for goodness' sake! He needed to stay with me for a couple of days and then he would be gone. If the police called, I was to tell them I had not heard from him."

"What happened?"

"Well naturally I told him not to be so foolish. That if the police wanted to talk to him, he should go to them, but he became almost hysterical, so I told him to come home."

"Is that what he did?"

"Yes. He was in a frightful state, sobbing like a little girl, half hysterical. I gave him a hot bath and a hot meal and that seemed to soothe him. He wanted to tell me some ridiculous story about a girl who had been killed, and somebody who was trying to frame him. I didn't want to hear it and I told him so."

I frowned. "But when the police telephoned you..."

"I told them what I told you: I had nothing to say. Our family business is none of your concern. I am only talking to you, Detective Stone, because you threatened me."

"Where is he now, Ms. Browne?"

"I have already told you I don't know. He stayed a couple of days, then flew to somewhere in Europe. He didn't want to tell me where, and frankly his behavior was so absurd I didn't want to know."

Dehan was making a face like brain-ache. "But everything he told you was true."

Mary gave her head a stiff little shake. "You don't know Cyril. He is always making up absurd stories and getting ridiculously emotional over them."

Dehan gave a small laugh and shook her head too. "No, Ms. Browne. What he told you was true. Do you not understand that?"

Her cheeks flushed. "Don't try to tell me about my own brother! I *know* what he is like! Before long, he'll come running back because he has wet his pants, or grazed his knee, and I will have to bathe him and cook him a meal and then he'll cry himself to sleep like a silly little girl. He is hopeless."

I gave Dehan a glance to shut her up and asked, "What is the age difference between you, Ms. Browne?"

"What has that to do with anything?"

"Please answer the question."

"I am ten years his senior."

"Are you blood relations?"

"Of course we are! What an absurd question!"

"Ms. Browne, we are nearly done. Please bear with us a little longer. Can you tell me about your parents?"

She faltered, shrugged, gave her head another little shake. "I mean . . . like what?"

"Well, for example, they left you a substantial inheritance. You're a schoolteacher, he was a librarian, they are not the best-paid jobs in the world, yet . . ."

She cut me dead. "Both of our parents died when I was fifteen and Cyril was just five. The house was paid for, and both Mother and Father had substantial life insurance. By the time the authorities had finished messing around, I had turned sixteen. They put us through hell in the courts, trying to take Cyril away from me. But I fought them every step of the way, and in the end the judge decided we had been through enough, and it would do Cyril more harm than good to be placed with a foster family. So I brought him up on my own. They appointed us a social worker, but it didn't take me long to get rid of her."

I looked around the room and gestured with my hand. "I don't see any pictures of your parents, or of Cyril."

"They were good, strict Catholics. They didn't encourage sentimentality. Love and devotion should be for God. I brought Cyril up in the same way."

"Where in Europe did he go?"

"I told you I don't know. I don't *want* to know. He'll come back soon enough."

"Where in Europe *would* he go?"

"I don't *know!*"

Dehan said, "Why would he choose Europe? He must have had a reason to go there. Was there some place he always wanted to visit? There must be some reason he went there."

"How many times do I need to tell you? *I don't know!* When he was small he never stopped yammering. I spent my whole time telling him to shut up. And when he turned twelve you couldn't get him to utter a word. I don't know why he went to Europe, or where he went in Europe, and frankly I don't want to know because it is just another one of his *stupid* fantasies!"

I scratched my chin. "'Another one of his fantasies.' Did he have a lot of fantasies?"

"All the time."

"Can you give us an example?"

"More? How about moving to New York? Or his idea he was going to be 'independent'? Or that he would have a family of his own? The notion that he had been framed for murder, flying off to Europe. Why do you think I simply stopped listening to him? Every word that came out of his mouth was some kind of stupid fantasy."

Dehan sighed and sat forward, with her elbows on her knees. The gesture was loud in the silent house. "Do you keep his bedroom ready for him to return?"

She shrugged. "It's his bedroom."

"Has he anything in there like a hairbrush from which we might be able to get a sample of his DNA?"

"Certainly not!"

"Certainly not, you won't let us, or certainly not, there is nothing of that sort?"

"Certainly not, there is nothing of the kind. This is a clean, respectable house, Detective. Do you honestly think I would have a dirty hairbrush hanging around for *twelve years*?"

Dehan sighed again and muttered, "Certainly not."

"I should think not."

I said, "Would you allow us then, Ms. Browne, to take a sample of DNA from you? We would be able to establish from that whether the samples at the scene were from a relative of yours."

"Not," she said, "under any circumstances whatsoever. And if you have finished with your *absurd* questions, I would now like you to leave. This ridiculous situation has gone on far too long. Now, please." She stood. "Leave, and leave me and my family alone!"

I sat watching her a moment, then stood. She was almost as tall as I was. Dehan stood too, and I said, "How did your parents die, Mary?"

"It was a car crash. Why?"

"Did Cyril witness it?"

She hesitated before answering. "He was in the car, if you must know. What is this, some psychological nonsense? God saw fit to take them. We accept His will and get on with it."

I offered her a sad smile and nodded, like I knew what she was talking about only too well. "Sure. Thank you for your time, Ms. Browne. I am sorry if we've brought up distressing memories." I pointed at the embroidery on the sofa. "That is quite lovely."

She was taken aback. "Oh, thank you."

I laughed. "You'll think me stupid, but I have a small request. I have had a splinter in my finger since yesterday. I can't seem to get rid of it. I wonder if I could borrow your needle . . ."

"Oh, good heavens! Of course!"

She reached for her sewing basket, but I stepped over and

removed the needle from her hoop and put it in my pocket. "Thank you so much. You have been extremely helpful and kind. My apologies once again for disturbing you. We'll see ourselves out."

We stepped back out into the gentle Californian sunshine and closed the door behind us. We walked back toward the car. It bleeped loudly as we approached, and Dehan asked me, "So that was weird. You want me to pick out that splinter for you?"

I stood staring across the road and shook my head. "No, thanks..."

"So what do we do now?"

"We go to church, Dehan. We go to church and pray for guidance..."

NINE

Across the road from Mary Browne's house was the school where she taught. Next door to it, and apparently attached, was the Good Shepherd Catholic Church. It was huge, and set in the middle of a large parking lot, resembling more a vast, modern conference center than the traditional idea of a church.

We crossed the road, and then the parking lot, and pushed through the large plate glass doors into a cool, shaded reception area with high ceilings and marble floors. There was a desk, with leaflets on it, and behind the desk there was a smiling woman in a dark blue suit. I returned her smile and said, "I never saw a church with a receptionist before."

"This *is* the twenty-first century! And after all, isn't St. Peter heaven's receptionist?"

Dehan made a noise that might have been a laugh but sounded more like a gurgle. I said, "I had never thought of it like that. I was wondering if we could have a talk to whoever is in charge . . ."

Her eyes twinkled with religious humor. "I think the Lord might be a little busy at the moment, but I'll see if Father Cohen is free."

I watched Dehan's eyebrow climb all the way up to her hairline. "Father Cohen?"

The woman beamed. "Do you know him?"

Dehan shook her head. "No, I never met a Father Cohen before."

She picked up an internal phone and said, "Whom shall I say . . . ?"

I showed her my badge. "I'm Detective Stone, and this is Detective Dehan, we are here making some inquiries about a case in New York. We would like to ask Father Cohen a couple of questions about a parishioner of his."

She made an O with her mouth, put the phone down, and tapped across the large, echoing reception to disappear through a couple of doors at the far end. Dehan said, "I guess there is no reason why not."

"None at all."

"You could have a rabbi called O'Malley, couldn't you?"

"Or an atheist called Dehan."

We stood in silence for a moment, and I had the strange sensation that even the silence was echoing in the vast space. After a moment Dehan whispered, "What are we doing here?"

I whispered back, "Trying to understand."

"In a church?"

I nodded, and the doors across the echoing hall opened again and the receptionist reappeared, accompanied now by a tall man in his sixties with curling red hair not yet turning to gray and a vigorous stride. He was dressed in jeans with a checked shirt and walked toward us smiling, with his hand held out. It was a gesture he had to abandon halfway because it was such a long distance to cover before he got to us. When he did arrive, he stuck out his hand again and shook mine, then Dehan's.

"Father Cohen," he said. "And you must be Detectives Stone and Dehan. A pleasure to welcome you to our humble home. I was just about to take my morning constitutional; will you walk with me in the gardens?"

We said we would and stepped out of the church, back into the sunlight. We crossed the road and entered onto a large common, fringed by trees and dotted here and there with occasional benches. Once on the grass, he slowed his pace and said, "So, how can we help the NYPD?"

Dehan said, "We are trying to locate Cyril Browne."

He stopped dead in his tracks and frowned at her. "Why don't you speak to his sister? She lives right here."

He gestured at her house. I scratched my chin. "We have. Father, if I could explain . . . Some years ago, Cyril became the prime suspect in a murder case."

His eyes went wide, and he stared at me as though he thought I was insane. "That is the single most absurd thing I have ever heard in my life. Forgive me."

I nodded. "I know. It's a long story. Just trust me that at the time, the evidence was compelling. However, my partner and I have uncovered new evidence that would seem to exonerate Cyril. The point is we do need to talk to him."

He made a face and pulled his mouth down, shaking his head. "This is all news to me. I am afraid if you think I can tell you where he is, you are barking up the wrong tree. I have had no contact with Cyril for years."

"No," I said. "I imagined as much. But Mary told us that about twelve years ago Cyril flew to Europe. She doesn't know where, or why for that matter, and she says she has not heard from him since."

"I see." He was frowning down at his feet as he walked, and sounded as though he really didn't see at all. "But I am sorry, I am still at a loss as to how you think I can help."

Dehan was squinting at me as though she agreed with Father Cohen. I plowed on.

"I don't believe Cyril stayed in Europe. I don't see how he could have. He had to have come back by now."

"That seems reasonable."

"So what I am trying to do is develop some kind of understanding about how Cyril thinks, what makes him tick, so that ultimately I can get some notion of where he is likely to have gone. I'm afraid his sister was not very helpful..."

He nodded that he understood. "Hmmm..."

"But if I can understand what makes Cyril tick, how he thinks, what things are important to him, what motivates him, like I say, maybe I can narrow my search down from the whole world, to places in the U.S.A. where he is most likely to have gone."

Father Cohen stopped and stared up at the sky, like he was asking his boss what the hell he thought he was playing at, sending this bozo to spoil his constitutional. "Gosh," he said. "That is a tall order."

"No," I said. "It's not really. I think there is one, defining event in Cyril's life that shapes and conditions everything he does."

They both stared at me and Dehan said, "His parents' death."

I nodded and asked Father Cohen, "Did you know them back then?"

"I had just left the seminary. I was about twenty-five. I grew up around here. That's why I requested this posting. The church is only twenty-five years old, and when they started construction, I spoke to the bishop..." He waved a hand at me. "But you don't want to know about all that. My point is that we, my family, we knew the Brownes. Most everyone knows each other around here. My father had married a Catholic girl from the neighborhood and we all—well, if we weren't friends, we were acquainted.

"They were good people, very devout. Old school." He nodded after he said it, as though confirming that old school was a good thing. "I can't say that I knew them well enough to give you a psychological insight into Cyril, but I do remember the accident. It was tragic."

"I believe he was in the car."

He studied my face a moment and looked vaguely queasy. We had reached the center of the common and he stopped. "Yes," he said, "but I'm afraid there is more to it than that. Shall we sit a moment?"

He gestured at a bench a few paces away by a small copse. We moved to it and sat. He took a deep breath and started to speak.

"Peter was the father. He was a strong man in every sense. Mary takes after him. They were very alike. But above all, his faith was strong. He was somewhat severe in his ways, but he was devoted to God and to his family. He worked hard and provided well for them. His wife was . . ." He sighed a sigh that was full of regret. "His wife, Marion, was charming, vivacious, happy, but of very poor judgment. And Peter—well, Peter hadn't the imagination, the wisdom, what you will—he lacked the *smarts*, if you like, to provide her with the kind of joyful life she needed. We are all different, and where his frugal, Spartan existence was enough to fulfill him, it was not enough for her, and we all watched her wilt. She needed, poor woman, just a little more joy in her life.

"Sadly, tragically, she met a man who was only too willing to provide that joy. She began to see him while Peter was at work and the children were at school. This man, I forget his name, worked on the local paper. He was a man of few morals, and the few he had he tended to neglect. He spent much of his time in bars and worked often from home. So Marion began to visit him there, at home—would that it had been in the bars! May God forgive me for saying so!"

He fell silent, looking at the trees and up at that perfect blue sky. Eventually he gave his head a small shake. "Marion didn't drink. They were both teetotal, she and Peter. But on that fateful afternoon, this man had encouraged Marion to have a drink, and she had yielded. One drink led, as it so often does, to another, and she had become drunk. She lost track of time, and the time to return home and collect the children from school had come and gone. Thank the Lord Mary was of an age to have her own key. She was a sensible, responsible girl, she collected her brother and saw him safely to the house.

"At five thirty, Peter returned home and found that his wife was not there. These were the days before everybody had a cell phone. He came to the church, assuming she was here, but nobody here had seen her, and so he went to his neighbors next door. There, his longtime friend told him bluntly that his wife was having an affair and she was at that very moment no doubt at this man's apartment. I don't know if what his friend did was right or not, but we had all suffered too long in silence watching him being cuckolded.

"Peter went insane. Why he put young Cyril in the car, we shall never know. Perhaps he thought he should not leave the children alone. Mary stayed with the neighbors. Why not Cyril? Perhaps he had it in his mind to hold up to her the full extent of her treachery, to shame her, to 'guilt-trip' her, in the modern usage. Whatever the case, he took Cyril and went to this man's apartment.

"There, on the sidewalk, in full view of everybody, he screamed at his wife, called her a . . . Called her names I shall not repeat, but which you can imagine. Then he physically manhandled her into the car. She, for her part, was screaming at him that he wasn't a man, that he was a sissy, that she was sick of him, all manner of horrible things. Then they took off at high speed, went across an intersection without stopping at the lights, and were rammed from the side by a truck. They were both killed instantly, and the boy witnessed the whole thing from the back seat."

We sat for a moment without speaking. There was quiet, sporadic birdsong in the trees above my head.

"You tell it as though you witnessed it."

"There were a handful of us who followed him. We were afraid of what he might do, that he might do something he would later regret . . ."

"You were here in Elk Grove? That's quite a coincidence."

"Oh, no, not at all." He smiled. "We have a long tradition in my family of spending Halloween together. It's quite a thing around here. I omitted to mention, it was Halloween. That's why he initially came to the church. He thought she might be helping out..."

I sat staring at the grass between my feet. Dehan stood and walked away with her hands in her pockets. Father Cohen frowned at her and then at me. "Is that significant?"

I smiled. "It might be."

"I'm sorry, I don't know what else to tell you."

Dehan had started walking in a wide circle, staring down at her boots. On a sudden impulse, I said, "His mother, Marion, she didn't quite fit in. She wasn't from the neighborhood, was she?"

"Oh, no. No, she wasn't."

Dehan had stopped and was watching me with narrowed eyes. I sighed. Father Cohen was frowning at me. I said, "She was a New Yorker, wasn't she?"

"Well, in a sense, yes. Her family hailed from the Bronx. But they had moved west when she was young. I forget where they went to. It wasn't far from here. Oh, yes!" He snapped his fingers. "Reno. She spent most of her childhood in Reno, then they moved to Sacramento and finally Elk Grove. Apparently the crime rate in Reno was quite high, and they were looking for a better environment for their daughter. Tragic how it played out in the end. Tragic, and not a little ironic."

I thought for a moment, sucking my teeth. "What paper was it that this guy worked on?"

"The *Elk Grove Herald*. They ran the full story, which must have been very distressing for Mary. The journalist was fired and left town, I believe. I can't imagine that any of this is very helpful to you, Detective."

Dehan was still staring at me. I said, "More than you can imagine, Father. You have actually been extremely helpful."

We left him finishing his morning constitutional and crossed the common back toward Mary's house. The birds were still chattering but seemed too lazy to get a real conversation going. As we approached the car, Dehan stopped in her tracks and spread her hands. "*Halloween?* Seriously? He sees his parents killed on Halloween? What are the odds, Stone? There is no way that is a coincidence."

I pressed the button on the key fob and the car bleeped. "So if it isn't a coincidence, how do you explain it?"

"I can't. It can't be done." She approached the car and got in, slamming the door. "This case is full of meaningless coincidences. Coincidences that don't mean anything."

I laughed. "That would be a meaningless coincidence."

"And you want to tell me how you knew that his mother was from New York?"

"I could smell another meaningless coincidence."

I pressed the ignition and pulled away, turned left onto Foulks Ranch Drive, and then left again onto Elk Grove Boulevard. Dehan scowled.

"Where are we going?"

"As soon as you find it on your phone, the public library."

She did a lot of swiping and typing and after a moment said, "It should be coming into view right about now. It's on the crossroads."

We were approaching a large intersection that looked more like a few buildings scattered in a woodland than the heart of a town, but this was the center of Elk Grove, and on the far side, on the right, was a large, modern building that claimed to be Elk Grove's public library.

"You going to do another one of those things where you don't tell me anything? Why are we at the public library?"

"Not at all, Dehan." I pulled over and parked. "We are at the public library because I want to have a look at these people. I figure if they ran a full report on the incident, then there is probably a photograph of the Browne family."

"Yeah, okay, I kind of got that, but why? What do you want to see a photograph of them for? Where is your mind going, Stone?"

I stared out the windshield and sighed. "I need to see them, get a feel for them. How are we going to find out where Cyril is, if we haven't got a sense of *who* Cyril is?"

I climbed out of the car and started toward the entrance to the library. I heard the door slam behind me and Dehan mutter, "I know where my mind is going. Out of itself."

TEN

We had sat in the quiet, spacious library, with the gentle, California light leaning in through the tall windows, making long, glistening ghosts out of the dust particles that lingered in the air. Now and then a distant echo would disturb the silence: a muffled cough, a book dropped on a table in another part of the building, a door opening briefly to allow in the hum of a passing car. Dehan had sat next to me, leaning against me with one arm on my shoulder, and we had read the article together. It didn't add anything to what Father Cohen had told us already, except the name of the journalist, Jose Rodriguez, who had been summarily dismissed following the incident.

There had been several photographs of the family as a whole and of the individuals that comprised it. They, the family, were described in the article as God-fearing, long-standing members of the community. The journalist had managed to imply that Marion's childhood in Reno was somehow responsible for her lamentable behavior, and that though her death was a tragedy, the kids were somehow, in the long run, better off without her. The real shame was that Peter had not survived with them.

I had stopped reading after a while and sat staring at the photographs. There was a close-up of Cyril, aged five. He had dark hair and sad eyes in a gaunt face. He was thin and boney, and you somehow got the feeling he was sensitive. Books would definitely have figured in his life, and I wondered if in different circumstances he might not have become a poet.

Mary, his sister, had been prettier back then, when she was younger. She gazed, smiling out of her portrait photo, as though toward a happy future. Even then, at fifteen, there was a strength about her, both physical and of character, a determination perhaps that any sign of weakness would be labeled "nonsense" or a "fantasy," and dismissed. I guessed that was how she dealt with her own loss and grief. That was the way she stayed strong.

A third photograph showed the whole family in their backyard. Cyril was in the foreground, on a tricycle, squinting at the camera in the sun. Mary was standing behind him, holding her father's arm in both of hers. There was something proprietary about the gesture, which he echoed by placing his hand gently on her forearm. Like him, she was tall, with a strong, heavy body. He didn't smile at the camera; rather, he seemed to assess it and judge it through narrowed eyes. His wife, Marion, stood slightly apart from them, resting her backside on a garden table. She had a pair of aviator sunglasses perched on her head. Like her son, she was squinting at the camera, half smiling. The similarity with her daughter was striking, except that she was of a finer build, more delicate, like her son. Mary had inherited her father's physical strength and "big bones," Cyril his mother's sensitivity.

I had sat like that, staring at them, for a good fifteen minutes, letting my mind roam and wander, until Dehan nudged me and said, "What now, Sensei, you want to grab a coffee?"

I glanced at my watch. It was eleven o'clock. "Let's go and have lunch in Reno."

Her eyes went wide and her jaw set. "See?" She said it loudly and it echoed. "You're doing it! You *are!*"

Somebody went, "Shshsh!" and Dehan repeated in a hoarse whisper, "*You are doing it, Stone! Tell me why we are going to Reno!*"

I grinned. "In the car. And if you can't learn to behave, this is the last time I bring you to the library."

"Funny. You're really funny."

We left amid scowls and returned to the car. I threw her the keys and climbed in the passenger seat, and as she got behind the wheel I said:

"I don't know, Dehan. I'm kind of groping in the dark, but like you said, these coincidences can't *be* coincidences: his mom's from the Bronx, she's killed on Halloween, he disappears on Halloween, Sue dies on Halloween . . ." I closed my eyes, trying to grasp a thought. "Somehow, in some way, he is trying to follow his mother. So, at the moment I am just following them."

She glanced at me and started the car. "Reno . . . ?"

"Uh-huh."

She pulled away. "What for?"

"You picked up, like I did, that Cyril felt oppressed and controlled by his sister, right?"

"Yeah, I got that."

She turned into Elk Grove Florin Road and we started moving north.

"Bear with me. I'm trying to fit my thoughts together here. It's like we have two camps: Mary and her dad, strong and controlling, knowing what's best for everybody and trying to keep order; and in the other camp Cyril and Marion, more sensitive, weaker in some ways, but needing to get away and be free. She breaks out by having an affair with a boozing, amoral journalist. He breaks free by physically escaping. In a sense he's following his mother's footsteps *backward*. Like he is trying to get her back, by going back *to* her somehow. Does that make any sense?"

She made a skeptical face. "Kind of . . ."

"When he tried to escape from his sister's control, get away from her, where did he go?"

"New York, where his mother was a kid. Okay, I get it. But it doesn't hold up, Stone. Sue died on Halloween. The same night his mother died. So is he trying to get back to her, or is he punishing her for abandoning him?"

I sighed and recited the facts for the thousandth time, trying to see the pattern hidden in them: "He disappears from New York and returns home in a panic, claiming he's being framed for Sue's murder. Framed by whom? And why? We don't know. Then he goes to Europe." I sucked my teeth a moment and gazed out at the pretty town that was slipping by. "I have a problem with that, Dehan. I am not sure, but I think he would've needed a visa to go to Europe. We need to look into that. But I do know for a fact that he couldn't just stay there. He would need papers, a work permit, all that. So he *must* have come back." I looked at her. "Where did he go? It's just a hunch, but it seems to me that, whether he is punishing her or trying to get back to her—or both—his mother plays a big part in his motivation. Did you happen to notice that there was a certain similarity between Xara, his sister, and his mother? Xara and his sister are bigger boned and heavier, but the likeness is there."

She had her bottom lip stuck out and she was nodding.

"Okay, Sensei, I hear you. So you think he might have gone to Reno."

"'Think' is putting it a bit too strongly. It's a hunch I'd like to explore."

She was quiet for a bit, then said, "We could sure use his financials right now."

I grunted. "I have a feeling we are going to find that Cyril Browne's financial records stop suddenly 'round about the time he left New York."

She looked at me sharply. "Based on what?"

I thought about it. "Based on his character, on his meticulous planning..."

"Planning? So you think he's the guy again?"

"I don't know yet who the guy is."

"Yet..."

"Let me think for a bit."

"You want a pipe and a violin?"

"That would be nice, thank you."

We didn't talk much after that. We rolled the windows down and enjoyed the gentle sunshine as we moved through Sacramento and then turned east and began the slow climb toward the Sierra Nevadas. All the way I kept turning my idea over and over. It was, as Mary would have said, absurd, a fantasy. Equally it made sense and equally it was impossible to prove.

Almost impossible to prove.

As we climbed higher, the temperature began to drop, and after about an hour we had to close the windows. Past Auburn, the landscape changed and we were suddenly surrounded by rich woodland rolling over peaks as far as the eye could see. And by the time we had passed Colfax, the I-80 had narrowed to one lane each way and the woodland had become a dense forest that seemed to close in and enfold us.

There, I snapped myself out of my reverie, pulled my cell from my pocket, found the number for the Washoe County sheriff, and called. After talking to a couple of people, I was eventually put through to Undersheriff Sarah Pfenninger.

"Good morning, Undersheriff Pfenninger. My name is Detective John Stone, I am with the NYPD. We are trying to track down a suspect in a murder investigation, we've been making inquiries in Sacramento, and we think our man may have been in Reno at some time. He may even still be there now."

"Okay, Detective Stone. How can we help?"

I tried to put a nice smile in my voice. "Well, first off, we don't want to tread on local law enforcement's toes. So this is partly a courtesy call."

"Much appreciated."

"But second, we'd like to know if the sheriff's department has any record of our man . . ."

"Where are you?"

"On the I-80, just going through Gold Run on the California side of the border."

"What's your man's name?"

"Cyril Browne, originally of Elk Grove."

"When do you think he was here?"

"Early November 2006, or sometime after that. Sorry I can't be more precise."

"You're about an hour out, a little more if you stick to the speed limit. You know where we are? 911 East Parr Boulevard. Put it in your SatNav. Ask for me at the front desk. I'll come down for you. Meantime, I'll make some inquiries. Send me a picture and I'll put out a BOLO."

"Thank you, Undersheriff, that is very . . ."

"What's your precinct, Detective Stone?"

"Forty-Third, in the Bronx. My commanding officer is Deputy Inspector John Newman."

"See you in an hour and twenty. Name's Sarah."

I hung up. Dehan looked at me along her eyes. "All good?"

I nodded once. "Very efficient woman." I spoke as I punched the address into the GPS. "She'll see us in an hour and twenty minutes. She's making inquiries and putting out a BOLO."

"Great. So what's wrong?"

I sent Pfenninger the photograph of Cyril, then sighed and shook my head. "I may be wrong . . ." I said. "We'll see when we get there. Don't ask me. It's a stupid idea. I just have a feeling . . ."

We arrived an hour and ten minutes later. The Washoe County Sheriff's Office is not what you would normally associate with a county sheriff. It is a huge, modular construction, set on the edge of the desert to the north of Reno, and looks more like a military HQ from a *Star Wars* movie than anything else. We left the car in the parking lot, went in to the front desk, gave the deputy our names, and, two minutes later, Undersheriff Sarah Pfenninger appeared in a khaki uniform with smartly tapping heels. She was short, sharp, and efficient, with very blond hair pulled back so tight you could almost hear it scream, and very blue eyes that didn't seem to care how much her hair screamed.

She greeted me and shook hands and regarded Dehan without expression.

"Your man popped up right away. Follow me."

We followed her down a passage, through a door and a busy detectives' room into an office that had three glass walls through which she could keep an eye on her troops. There she sat down, and we sat too. She said, "Can I see some ID?"

We showed her our badges and she sat back in her chair to look at us both.

"He's your suspect, but he's on my turf. What's the story with this guy?"

Dehan said, "He's a possible suspect in a murder inquiry."

They both looked at each other a moment. Pfenninger seemed to be waiting. After a moment, she raised her eyebrows. "Your partner already told me that. You want to put some skin on the bones?"

I filled her in with what we had found so far, and she listened carefully, with a small frown creasing her brow. When I'd finished, she said, "That's a pretty weird story. What's his motive for killing the girl?"

Dehan crossed one long leg over the other. "We don't know that he did. On the face of it, we just want to eliminate him from our investigation."

Pfenninger let her eyes rove over Dehan, seemed to find her wanting, and turned back to me. "You figure he's emotionally unstable."

"It's possible."

"Probable."

I nodded. "Probable."

"He has big issues with his mother. Could have killed your Sue Benedict out of jealousy."

I drew breath to answer but Dehan interrupted. "You said his name popped up right away."

Pfenninger looked at her for a full three slow seconds, with her fingers laced over her belly, before nodding.

"Yup."

I said, "He's dead, isn't he?"

Dehan looked at me in astonishment. Pfenninger raised an eyebrow at me. "How would you know that, Detective Stone?"

Dehan echoed her: "Yeah, Detective Stone, how would you know that?"

I sighed. "A hunch. How did it happen? Did he come here from Europe?"

"I don't know. You say he disappeared from New York in the early hours of November first, he showed up in Reno on November eighth."

"How do you know that?"

Her face was totally expressionless. "Keep listening and I'll tell you." I heard Dehan snort, but I ignored her. Pfenninger kept talking. "He was lodging at a house on the edge of the desert, Chablis Drive, out by the 395. Landlady said he was quiet. No trouble. Never spoke to nobody. Friday night, that's November tenth, two days after he arrived, he goes to a building site on the river, by East Second Street Bridge. They were putting up a big hotel-casino at the time, and they'd poured a load of concrete that day into the foundations. So your boy gets up on a big pile of rubble, just beside the wet cement, and starts screaming about how life don't have no meaning no more. The night watchman come running over, shining his flashlight, and he hears a big splash. Your boy had just jumped into the foundations. Wet concrete sucks you down like a quicksand. There ain't no way out of that. So that's where he's buried, in the foundations of the East Second Casino Hotel."

I frowned. "How do you know it was him?"

She gave a small sigh. "How many suicides have you dealt with over the years, Stone?"

I nodded. "A few."

"Jumpers off bridges? You got some nice jumping bridges in New York."

Dehan said, "I know where you're going. It's true. They always take their damn jackets off."

"Yup." She looked at Dehan and nodded. "Took his jacket off and left it lying on the rubble."

I was shaking my head. "I don't understand. Why didn't you notify his sister?"

"We didn't know he had one. When he registered here, he registered as having no next of kin. So there was nobody to notify."

Dehan said, "He turned up on the Wednesday, found lodgings, and the first thing he did was register?"

Pfenninger spread her hands. "What can I tell you? He was depressed, suicidal, maybe he was OCD, how should I know? From what you've told me, he was some kind of crazy."

I puffed my cheeks and drummed my fingers on the arm of the chair. "You have been extremely helpful, Sarah. Can I trouble you for one more thing?"

"It ain't no trouble. Just my job."

"The night watchman..."

She opened a file and pulled out a slip of paper. "I figured you'd want to talk to him. He's in charge of security at the same hotel. Give him a call. He'll be happy to talk to you. His name's Joseph White. He's black. One of them ironies you was talking about."

We left her watching us leave through the glass walls of her office, with her fingers laced over her belly.

ELEVEN

The East 2nd Casino Hotel was a sprawling, four-story building in red brick and beige that stood directly opposite the Greater Nevada baseball field. I pulled into the underground parking lot, found a space, and we took the elevator up to the foyer. There was a lot of brown leather and red carpeting, and just past the reception desk on the right, a huge arch led to three broad steps that took you down into the ninth circle of hell, where all the fruit machines are.

Behind the reception desk there were a pretty young woman and a pretty young man, both in blue suits. He had a burgundy tie and she had a burgundy scarf. They both had very white teeth, which they displayed like badges of office.

"Good afternoon, my name is Sally. How can I help you today?" She said that.

I said, "We are police officers from New York. The sheriff's department tells me I can find Joseph White here. I believe he is head of security."

She picked up the internal phone, dialed three digits, and smiled at me with her head on one side while it rang.

"Mr. White? There are two detectives from New York here to

see you . . ." She held my eye while she listened and smiled, then said, "Okay, thank you," and hung up. "He'll be right down if you'd like to sit down, or have a few games in the casino, or have a refreshing cocktail in the Cavendish Cocktail Lounge."

We strolled over to a couple of brown leather armchairs and sat. I said, "It's amazing what they can do with artificial intelligence these days."

"She was definitely artificial, Stone, but intelligence . . . ?"

I snorted a laugh but didn't have time to answer, because a tall, athletic man in his sixties had entered the foyer from a broad staircase. He had hair graying at the temples, a dark blue, double-breasted blazer with brass buttons, and gray slacks. His black patent shoes were military clean, and he had a chest like a sherry cask. He glanced at reception, and AI Sally showed him her gleaming teeth and pointed at us. We stood as he approached. Dehan stuck out her hand as he made to reach for mine.

"Mr. White, I am Detective Carmen Dehan of the Forty-Third Precinct in New York. This is my partner, Detective John Stone. I wonder if you could spare us five minutes of your time to talk about Cyril Browne?"

He watched her carefully as she spoke, with a small frown on his brow. When she'd finished, he said, "Cyril who now?"

"Cyril Browne. The man who is part of the foundations of this building."

His eyebrows went up and his mouth made an O. He nodded. "Sure, sure. Let's go up to my office."

His office was a cubbyhole up a short flight of steps. There was no window, but he had a wooden desk, a black imitation leather chair, and two chairs for visitors. As he sat, he said, "Can I see some ID?"

We showed him and, as he handed them back, he asked Dehan, "What is it you want to know?"

"Can you tell us exactly what happened that night?"

He leaned back and sighed. "It's a long time ago, Detective. Ten, twelve years?"

"Twelve years last November. It's important, or we wouldn't have come all the way from New York."

He nodded. "I get that." His expression became abstracted and he seemed to study the edge of his desk. "It was the craziest suicide you could ever imagine. Still gives me nightmares from time to time." He looked up and frowned at her. "I just can't imagine a more horrible way to die."

I repeated Dehan's question. "What happened, Joe?"

He glanced at me, then back at his desk. "It was the first week of November, I guess. I don't recall the exact date . . ."

"The report says it was the tenth."

"Yeah, that's about right. This, what you see here, was just a building site. Early stages. They was just laying down the foundations. There were big heaps of rubble waiting to be taken away, big holes in the ground where they were laying the concrete for the foundations. It was a kind of organized chaos, if you know what I mean."

I smiled. "Sure."

"So in all that chaos, as I am sure you can understand, you had not only valuable tools and equipment, you also got the risk of some kid getting in here to drink or take drugs or whatever kids get up to, and getting hurt or injured in the process—or worse. Then the company got to pay out for occupier's liability, for not making the place safe enough. The world we live in, right? Kid is stupid and gets hurt, the company is liable. Always somebody else's fault."

"That's why they had you there."

"Every night, there was two of us. We took it in turns to do the rounds, make sure nobody snuck in to take nothing. So that night, must have been ten or ten thirty. I'm doing my rounds and all of a sudden I start hearing this screaming and shouting. Some kid is going crazy, screaming that life has no meaning no more, that it's all over, that he just wants to die.

"So I get on my radio and call Sam, and I am running, hell-bent for leather toward where I can hear the screaming. It was over . . ." He twisted around in his chair, pointing awkwardly. "At the north corner, just in from the road a bit. There was a fence up, and there was a big pile of rubble up against the wall, oh, I suppose six or eight feet high, and there was a kid standing on the top of the rubble. He had his jacket in his hand and he was shouting like a madman."

Dehan had gone quiet. I asked him, "What did you do?"

"Well, you can imagine that in the dark it wasn't easy to run, with all that stuff lying around, and them big holes in the ground. They was cordoned off all right, but you could still trip and have a nasty fall. And if you fell in the wet concrete, you was in real trouble. So I was going as fast as I could, shouting to him not to do nothing stupid, that that was wet concrete there, and at the same time trying to make sense to Sam on the radio."

"Where was Sam?"

"He was in the hut, keeping warm. He never saw nothing."

"Okay." I leaned forward with my elbows on my knees. "Let me just make sure I have this straight. This young man was standing in the northwest corner of the site, on a pile of rubble, overlooking a pit that was filled with liquid concrete. Sam was in the hut, so he could see nothing, and you were trying your best to run to the boy, shout to him to be careful, talk on the radio, and shine your flashlight both on the boy and on the ground to make sure you didn't fall. You deserve a medal just for that, Joe. Where, exactly, were you when you were doing all this?"

He had started laughing. "It was a thing to behold, I can tell you. Where was I? As luck would have it, I was at the farthest point. Like you say, he was in the northwest corner, so I must have been in the southeast."

I sat back. "Okay, Joe, I have a clear picture in my mind now. What happened next?"

"Next thing, he just went and jumped in. Craziest thing I ever saw in my life. I can understand a man shooting his brains out. I can understand a man jumping in front of a train, or hanging hisself. Them's all quick deaths. Jumping off a building, get it over and done with. It's quick. But jumping into wet cement? There ain' no way anybody ever is gonna get you out of that. It's gonna get in your nose and mouth, and your eyes. That is gonna be one bad death. Like being in hell. And slow." He paused. His face was uncomprehending. His eyes were distressed. "I know the Mob used to do that a lot, but even them, you know? They'd kill you first."

We were quiet for a moment. Dehan was watching me curiously. I said, "Can you describe the boy to me, Joe?"

He blinked, pulling himself back from his nightmare. "Sure, he was kind of average height, maybe five ten, slim, dark hair. He was wearing dark pants and a dark sweater. That was about all I could see. He looked young, maybe late twenties or early thirties."

"Can you remember if he said anything in the moment he jumped?"

"Uh . . ." He stared at the wall. "It was kind'a crazy. He was screaming a lot, making a lot of noise. I was running, trying not to fall . . ." He shook his head. "No, he sort of went silent. Then there was this horrible splash and he was sinking into the cement."

"Then you scrambled up the rubble?"

"No. Sam arrived. I was pretty upset. He called the cops. They came about fifteen minutes later. There was no way to save the boy, though he must have took a whole minute or two to die. I was crazy, you know? Trying to find a stick or something to help pull him out. Cops started processing the scene and it was them found his jacket. Seems nuts, don't it? But the detective told me lots of suicides do that, before they jump, or before they drown themselves, take off their shoes and their jacket. Crazy."

"But he didn't take off his shoes."

"No, not his shoes, just his jacket." He studied my face for a bit. "Who was he?"

Dehan said, "Cyril Browne. A very unhappy young man." She hesitated, sighed, and said, "Joe, I know it's easy after all this time to trick yourself into remembering things that you either want to believe or think you ought to believe. So I want you to think very carefully, okay? It seems likely that Cyril either killed a woman in New York or was framed for her murder. His dying words could be really important. Can you remember with any degree of certainty what he was shouting?"

He seemed to sag in his chair. "Oh, Lord . . ." He was quiet for a long time, staring at that spot on his desk. "Life had no meaning anymore. I know he kept saying that. He was coming home. I remember he said that a couple of times. She was gone . . ." He hesitated. "I don't want to go inventing things, but he might have said he was going home to her. But I really don't want to say no more because that might be bullshit."

I looked at Dehan. She was thinking, frowning at the desk. The desk was getting frowned at a lot that afternoon. I said, "You have any more questions, Detective Dehan?"

She looked at me for a moment, her eyes flicking around my face. Then she shook her head. "No. No, I think that's everything."

I stood, leaned over, and shook his hand. "Thanks, Joe. We'll see ourselves out."

We made our way down in the elevator, into the dark, echoing parking garage. I pressed the key and our car bleeped. Dehan was looking down at the floor with an odd expression on her face.

"You think he's down there?"

I went and opened the driver's door, looked back at her where she was watching me. "If he is, I guess that constitutes concrete evidence that he's a hardened criminal."

She frowned. "That's not funny, Stone."

"I know. Get in the car, will you? I'm starving."

She walked toward me. "It's kind of funny, but your timing is awful."

She got in and we drove out into the bright, freezing afternoon. As we emerged from the garage, my phone pinged. It was an email. I pulled it from my pocket and handed it to her. "Have a look, will you?"

She swiped the screen a couple of times and said, "It's from the inspector." She glanced at me. "Cyril's financials." She looked back at the screen and spoke absently. "I guess they're pretty much irrelevant now."

After that, she was quiet for a while, reading, swiping occasionally, then reading some more.

"That's odd."

I glanced at her as I turned onto South Wells Avenue. "What is?"

She frowned out the windshield at the long road ahead. "He disappeared from New York in the early hours of November first. He showed up in Reno November eighth and killed himself November tenth."

"Yeah, so?"

"He booked a ticket on October fifteenth, flying from San Francisco to Geneva on November twelfth."

We were quiet for the length of the avenue. I turned right into Plumb Lane and then right again into a large shopping mall with a parking lot. There I saw a bar called Shenanigan's Old English Pub and decided the gods were smiling on me that day. I parked outside and we went in. Dehan was still reading Cyril's financial records on my phone.

I ordered two pints of best bitter and two Chicago beef melts. We found a table and sat. I put down the beers and she put down my phone, took a sip, and said, "There was no activity at all on his account, or his credit card, after November tenth."

I gave a nod. "There wouldn't be if he was dead. But we need to have a very close look at those records. What was the state of his account on the morning of the tenth?"

"One hundred and ten dollars."

I took a pull and wiped my mouth with the back of my hand. "He wasn't going very far on that in Geneva, was he?"

She stared at me awhile, half wincing, like her mind hurt. "What the hell was he planning to do in Geneva?"

"What is Geneva famous for, Dehan?"

"Banks . . . ?" She looked away. "What the hell was he up to?" I drew breath, but she held up a hand. "No, wait, I got this. Just let me think for a minute."

The waitress came with the beef melts, told us to enjoy, and went away. I was halfway through mine when Dehan looked at me and said, "He had built a whole damn fantasy in his mind. Like his sister said he did. You know what?" Her cheeks colored. "I could take Fernando and beat seven bales of shit out of that son of a bitch." She pointed at me. "Sue and Cyril didn't get close the night of the party. They were already getting close, but as friends. Anyone who managed to get below the surface with Cyril says the same thing: he was a nice guy. And Sue was a nice girl. And because of Fernando's interfering, they started to get to know each other. Trouble is, Cyril fell in love and built this big fantasy about her. He was planning something." She paused, staring at nothing. "He was smart, and I am willing to bet my next paycheck that he was planning some kind of heist, robbery, swindle—some smart way to make a lot of money. And in his fantasy, him and Sue were going to escape together to Switzerland, where he was opening, or had opened, a bank account. *That* is why he was going to Switzerland, and *that* is why there was practically no money in his account. Because he had already transferred it."

I spoke around a mouthful of food. "If I suggested something like that to you, you'd tell me it was a hell of a reach based on very little."

"Think about it, Stone. He hands in his notice at work, why? Because he won't need to work anymore. He hands in his notice with his landlord. Why? Because he won't need to live there anymore. He goes to Switzerland. Why? For the banks. His account, despite the fact that he is moving house, is empty! Why? Because he has transferred the funds to another account. I bet when I look at these records properly, I will find a large transfer just before Halloween 2006."

I nodded. "I am sure you will."

She finally picked up her melt. "And I'll tell you something else, that son of a bitch Fernando and his pal Giorgio killed Sue and framed Cyril. As far as I am concerned they may as well have put a gun to his head and shot him too. And they are going down for it."

TWELVE

We got back to Elk Grove at shortly before eight p.m. Dehan had managed to book two seats on a JetBlue flight out of Sacramento at just before midnight, landing at JFK at ten past eight in the morning, just five hours later. So we packed, had a light supper at the Little Buddha Thai restaurant, and tried to sleep the best we could on the plane.

The best we could was about three hours, and we climbed off next morning, in a dark, frozen, cloudy New York, feeling ragged and unhappy. We found the Jaguar in the parking garage where we had left it, and it whispered to me of home, of log fires and a long sleep on the sofa. I told Dehan what the Burgundy Beast had whispered to me and she frowned disapproval, first at me and then at my car. Her expression said we should meet with the inspector and decide on a strategy for proving Fernando and Giorgio's guilt. I pretended not to notice and unlocked the trunk.

It was as we were chucking our bags in that my phone rang. It was the inspector.

"Good morning, sir. I hope you had a good sleep. We managed a little less than three hours."

Dehan made a face that was scandalized and spread her hands

in a "what?" gesture. I shrugged, and the inspector said, "Where are you? Are you back yet?"

"We literally just this very moment got off the plane."

"Good. As soon as you get to the precinct, come up and see me."

"About eight tomorrow morning, sir?"

There was a long silence, then a slight wheezing noise. "Oh... I see... I didn't get it at first. Very funny. I didn't realize, John, that you had a sense of humor. Very good. I'll see you in about forty minutes." As he hung up I heard him mutter, "What a character..."

I slammed the trunk and climbed in behind the wheel. We drove in sleepy silence out of the airport complex, but as we were joining the Van Wyck Expressway headed north, Dehan, who was sitting with her arms crossed and her brows knitted, shifted in her seat to look at me. Outside, everything seemed to be various shades of gray, and frosted, like a Christmas cake smothered in soot.

"What's up?" she demanded. "That's not like you at all."

"What isn't?"

"Wanting to go home when we're wrapping up a case. Usually you're a pain in the ass who won't let anybody rest."

I made a face that suggested she was making a big deal out of very little. "I figure the case has been cold for twelve years, we can take a few hours to catch up on sleep."

But even as I was saying it, the words were troubling me. She was right. Something was nagging at my mind. Something that was not good. We sped past two large trucks that were spitting sludge and spray from their wheels and I became aware that I had started accelerating without realizing it. Dehan said:

"Wait a minute. You've... *son of a gun*! You solved it, didn't you? You know what happened!"

I glanced at her, only partly aware of what she was saying. After a while I said, "Yes..."

"When?"

"Yesterday, at the library. But there were things I needed to confirm. I confirmed them in Reno. But there is something troubling me, Dehan."

"Why didn't you tell me, Stone? It's not nice when you do this. We're supposed to share, you know?"

I nodded. Chewing my lip. "I know. I was wrong..."

"At least you can admit it. So tell me what happened."

"No, I mean I was wrong about the case. It's not finished yet. We need to... *Goddamn it!*"

I floored the pedal and hit 110 MPH through Queens, crossed the Bronx–Whitestone Bridge into Throggs Neck, and five minutes later, I was skidding to a halt outside the station house on Fteley Avenue. As we climbed the stairs to the inspector's office, Dehan said, "Okay, you scared me half to death by doing a hundred and ten in a sixty-eight-year-old car in the sleet and snow, now you want to tell me what the hell..."

I interrupted her. "Put it together, Dehan! Marion, Mary, Xara, Jose Rodriguez, Fernando..."

I ran up the remaining stairs. She called after me: "*What?*"

I called over my shoulder, "I can't explain now. There's no time!"

I knocked and pushed in without waiting for a reply. The inspector looked up from his desk. "Ah, John, Carmen..."

She was coming through the door. I said, "Is it Fernando Martinez?"

He frowned and blinked. Then his eyebrows arched. "Good Lord, John, how on Earth...?"

Dehan closed the door and said sourly, "Don't bother, sir. He won't tell you."

"Sit down, both of you, please. I am keen to hear about your trip to Sacramento... *and* Reno! But first I need to tell you. As you requested, I had Fernando Martinez and Giorgio Gonzalez run through the system to see if they had any priors out of state. Your hunch was good. Not Giorgio, but Fernando. He is wanted on several charges of violence against women, in Texas, New

Mexico, and Arizona. The offenses range from assault and assault with a deadly weapon to attempted rape and rape. His latest brush with the law was in New Jersey. A complaint was made by a prostitute at a club in Newark. She claimed he beat her up, but she later dropped the charges."

"I knew it!" Dehan balled her fist and punched me on the shoulder. "I *knew it*!"

The inspector made a face of bemusement and gave a small laugh. "There is the small matter of the DNA sample . . ."

She was already shaking her head. "We have a theory that could explain that, sir . . ."

"You have . . . ?"

He turned and watched me pull out my phone. I dialed. It rang once and Frank said, "I was about to call you."

"That's what they all say, but they never call. Listen, did you find anything on the semen distribution?"

I watched the inspector frown at Dehan. Frank said, "That's what I was going to call you about." I put him on speakerphone and placed the phone on the desk. "You have to understand that this is not enough to clinch a case, John. With other evidence, it can be persuasive. The fact is I did that autopsy myself. I don't remember it, but they are my notes. You're lucky I am thorough in my work, and I did notice that the semen was not pooled at the end but, in fact, smeared around the walls of the vagina. Now, that can be caused by several things, amongst them very energetic or athletic intercourse. However, it *is* consistent with the scenario you proposed, where semen collected in a condom is then introduced into the victim's vagina in order to frame somebody else."

There was a moment's silence. "Thanks, Frank. I understand. I'll be in touch."

He hung up, and we sat staring at the inspector, who sat staring back at us. After a moment, he heaved a deep sigh and slumped back in his chair. Dehan said, "We should contact some of his victims, see if they'll talk to us. We might get something from them."

He slid the file across the desk to her. "Talk to Melanie Delano in Jersey. I'm not sending you to New Mexico."

We stood, and I opened the door. As I was about to step out, the inspector said, "John? Carmen? Sooner or later there has to be a case that just can't be cracked..."

Dehan nodded, but I frowned. "Oh, I've cracked it, sir. I know who did it: how and why. I just need to prove it."

Halfway down the stairs, Dehan said, "It's Fernando, right?"

"We need the evidence, Dehan. Call Melanie, will you? Arrange to see her this morning. We'll drive over to Jersey, but I want to pass by Giorgio's place first."

We stepped out into the freezing, blustery wind again and made our way toward the car on unsteady feet while Dehan dialed. As we climbed in, she spoke suddenly in a bright, friendly voice. "Hi! Is that Melanie? Hi! It's so nice to talk to you! Listen, you were recommended to me by a friend...?"

She gave the statement the intonation of a question. I rolled my eyes and fired up the beast. As we rolled out onto Story Avenue, she was saying, "She said you provided *special* services..." She squealed with laughter and curled up. "*I know! Right?* So I would like to book a session? For me and my husband...?" Another squeal of laughter. "Life's too short! Right? Can you see us later this morning? I'll pay extra for the short notice. It's his birthday and I just know... You will? Eleven thirty? Oh you are a *doll*! Thank you so *much*! Can't wait!" She hung up and grinned.

I shook my head. "Who are you? You scare me sometimes."

"I *know*! Right?" She chortled, and after a moment said, "Okay, partner, come clean. What was all that about Marion, Mary, Xara, Jose Rodriguez... How was any of that an answer to my question?"

I turned onto Soundview Avenue and began to accelerate south.

"You know the way ninety-nine percent of cases are all about sex?"

"I'd say a bit less, but yes."

"This one is, in some ways, no different. It is all about sex, but it is Freudian sex."

"Freudian sex . . . ?"

"Yeah, this is all about Cyril's mother."

She sighed, took hold of her long hair, and tied it into a knot behind her head. Then she sucked her teeth. Then she sighed again. "Okay, go on."

"Every woman in this case is, to a greater or lesser extent, a reflection of Cyril's mother . . ."

"Okay, maybe, but how does that help? And how does it clinch who killed Sue, or tell us why or how? Besides, Stone, I very much doubt that Fernando or Giorgio knew anything about Cyril's mother. And *also*, how does Jose Rodriguez come into it?"

I turned onto Thieriot Avenue. "See? If you had listened instead of talking, I might have had time to explain. But we're here now, so it will have to wait."

"Dork."

I turned into Lacombe and drove down Taylor Avenue, to pull up outside Giorgio's place. Then I leaned on the horn for ten seconds, which, if you count them out, is a long time to lean on a horn. By the time I'd finished, Dehan was staring at me like I had lost my mind. "What the hell are you doing?"

I smiled. "Announcing our arrival."

That didn't change her expression. She climbed out of the car and I followed. Giorgio was watching us from his window. We climbed the steps to his porch and he opened the door.

"That's a lot of noise you're making there. What can I do for you, Detectives?"

"I just have a couple of questions for you, Giorgio. You told us you were with three prostitutes the night Sue was killed."

"So what?"

"It was a lie, wasn't it?"

He didn't answer. He just watched me.

"So, what I would like to know is, did you hire the prostitutes for Cyril?"

His eyes narrowed but he still didn't say anything.

I gave him a moment longer and said, "Okay, how about Fernando and his record of violence against women? Do you participate or just try to cover for him and protect him?"

"Are you arresting me on some charge?"

"Not yet, but these are questions you will have to answer sooner rather than later. These and others." I placed my finger on his chest. "And take my advice, Giorgio. One of these days, there is going to be a knock at your door. Trick or treat. You better be ready."

I went down the steps back to the car and, across the road, I saw Sandy Beach looking out of her window at us. I turned to Dehan, who was still looking at me like I'd lost my mind. "Just give me a minute, will you? I'll be right back."

I crossed the road and pushed through Sandy's gate onto the path that led to her front door. It opened before I got there. She was smiling. "Hello, Detective. I couldn't help noticing you outside Giorgio's house. Is there something I can do for you?"

"I don't know, Ms. Beach. It's a long shot, but we're kind of against the ropes. We're a little concerned about Fernando, you know, Giorgio's friend?"

She frowned. "Yes, I know him slightly. Concerned about him why, Detective?"

"I can't really discuss the details, ma'am, but have you noticed any comings and goings at the house? Any women who might be . . ."

She gave a little gasp. "You mean . . . *pro*fessional?"

"Yes, exactly."

"Goodness . . . ! No, I can't say I have. They *do* have rather rowdy parties sometimes, but since I had a word with Giorgio, they seem to have moderated a bit."

"Can I give you my card . . ." I pulled one from my pocket and handed it to her. "And if you notice anything odd, we are particularly interested in Fernando, perhaps you could give me a call."

"Of course."

"In fact, can I have your number?" I pulled out another card and gave her my pen. She hesitated a moment, then wrote down her number on the back of the second card and handed it and the pen back to me. "I am very grateful, Ms. Beach."

"Sandy, please. Ms. Beach makes me sound so old!" She laughed, then became serious. "Giorgio isn't in any trouble, is he, Detective? I confess I have become rather attached to him."

I looked back at the house. Dehan had gotten back in the car. I could see Giorgio's form at the window, watching me. I said, "It's Fernando we are mainly interested in, Sandy, but my advice to you would be to keep your distance." I looked her in the eye. "Off the record, don't get involved with them. They are dangerous men."

There was real sadness in her eyes. "They're always either married or bastards, aren't they?" she said.

I gave a small laugh. "Often they're both, and that's just the women. The men are worse."

She laughed and slapped my arm. I said goodbye and returned to the car. I got behind the wheel and called the inspector. "Sir, can we have a discreet watch on Giorgio and Fernando for the next twenty-four hours?"

"If you're sure we need it, of course."

"I'm sure, sir. Maybe Santos and Clay, and Warren and Groves. They're good and reliable."

"Very well. Anything I need to know?"

"No, sir, not just yet. But tell them to be very discreet, very alert, and ready for the unexpected. We're on our way to Jersey. We'll be in touch."

I turned the key in the ignition and moved north up Taylor Avenue, back toward Soundview.

Dehan sighed. "Jersey?"

"No. Not yet. First, we are going to see Frank. Then our lady of the midmorning."

"Why Frank? Is there any point in my asking?"

"Yes, of course. Frank because I am increasingly worried about Fernando and Giorgio. They are dissolute, dangerous men."

She closed her eyes and crossed her arms. "You are *so* annoying!"

"I promise I will explain everything on the way to Jersey. Scout's honor."

I didn't tell her I was never a Scout.

THIRTEEN

The visit to Frank took less than five minutes, and Dehan stayed in the car, sulking. I ran in, had a brief chat with him, and trotted back out again, trying not to fall. Dehan was behind the wheel. I had a private chuckle with myself and got in the passenger side.

"It was either this, to work off my frustration, or beat you to death with my fists."

I laughed. "You made the right choice. The other could take a long time."

She turned the key. The big engine growled and we took off down Morris Park Avenue like she was after the kid who just took her baby brother's lunch money. I gave her a moment and said, tentatively, "You want me to tell you . . ."

"No."

"Come on, Dehan. Don't get mad."

"I'm not mad."

"Your face is mad."

"Thanks."

We drove in silence for a couple of minutes. Eventually, I said, "You're my partner, Dehan. I have to tell you my theory," and regretted it immediately.

Her face flushed and her eyes went bright. She glared at me. "No kidding!"

"Eyes on the road."

"Well, I don't want to know your theory! I will work it out for myself!"

"That is childish."

"Just keep going, buster."

She turned left into White Plains Road, over the bridge, and left again onto East Tremont. A couple more savage turns put her onto the East 177th access to the I-95, headed west.

"Are we really going to have a fight over this?"

"No."

"Can I tell you my theory then?"

"No. You wanted to keep it all to yourself. You keep it all to yourself."

"Watson wasn't like this," I said, and gave her a tentative smile.

"I, for your information, Mr. Stone, am *not* Watson!"

"Okay, you made your point. I apologize. It was vain and stupid of me. I just wanted to get the evidence before I committed to it."

"I am your partner. Aside from being your wife, I am your partner. We share our thoughts. That is what partners do. I am not some damned foil for your admittedly brilliant mind. Partner. *Comprende?*"

"Comprendo. I will strive to correct this flaw in my character. *Now* can I tell you?"

"Apology accepted. No, you can't. I am going to work this out for myself to prove to you that I am not Dr. John Stupid Watson."

I sighed. "Fine . . ." After a while I grinned. "It really is very, very subtle."

She looked at me with hooded eyes and said nothing. I followed her lead.

Thirty minutes later, we turned into Madison Street, found a spot in the high fifties, parked, and went to ring the doorbell.

When Melanie opened the door, Dehan gave me a look which involved arching her eyebrows high on her forehead. Melanie was pretty, of medium height and build, with long, blond hair. She could have been Sue's younger sister.

Dehan smiled. "Melanie? We spoke on the phone about an hour ago?"

Melanie beamed. "Oh, sure!" She smiled at me and winked. "Happy birthday, birthday boy! Come on in."

We stepped over the threshold into a small entrance hall. Before she could close the door, I said, "Melanie, there is something I need to tell you before we go any further."

She paused with her hand on the door and looked worried. "What?"

I pulled out my badge and showed it to her. "I am Detective John Stone, and this is my partner, Detective Carmen Dehan. We need to talk to you."

She kind of sagged against the door. "Oh, *man* . . ."

It was Dehan who answered. "The good news is we're not Vice, this is not our patch, and this is not a bust. We're from the Forty-Third in the Bronx."

Melanie frowned. "So what do you want, a freebie?"

I laughed. "No, thank you. We just want to ask you some questions. Talk to us and in ten minutes we'll be gone."

She sighed and closed the door. "Let's go up to my boudoir." As she climbed the stairs ahead of us, she said, "Bronx? I sure hope this ain't nothin' to do with that Fernando. I ain't gonna testify against that son of a bitch."

She led us into a small room with a sofa, a couple of brown vinyl chairs, and a huge TV on the wall. Dehan sat with her back to the door and Melanie draped herself on the sofa, facing Dehan. I took the other chair and let Dehan do the talking.

"Melanie, we are not asking you to testify. We are investigating a murder: the murder of a young woman who was very much like you. At the moment, all we are doing is putting the pieces together to try and get a picture of what happened the night she was killed. Now, what you can tell us could make all the difference between a killer going free, and killing again, or that killer being put away for life, where he can never hurt another woman. *Or* it could save an innocent man from going to prison. So it is really important, Melanie, that you be really honest with us and tell us exactly what happened between you and Fernando. You don't need to testify, and he will never know you spoke to us. Deal?"

She sounded like a kindly mother talking to a troubled child. I turned to look at Melanie. She was fiddling with the hem of her blouse. She raised her eyes to meet Dehan's.

"You better believe I am not going to testify. You put me in court and I will say he is the kindest, gentlest man on Earth."

"I understand that. What happened?"

"About six months ago, it was in the summer, he was over here with some pals of his. I was working at the Unholy Chapel, the nightclub on Chapel Street? I was serving tables, keeping company with the patrons, you know the kind of thing." She opened her eyes wide and laughed. "It's damn good money, I can tell you *that* for nothin'! And Tony? The boss? People say he's, like, an animal? But actually I think he's a real sweet guy. He never done nothin' to me, 'cept give me a chance to get on, and make some money."

"So Fernando was at the club that night?"

"Uh-huh, him and some friends of his. They was there having fun, spending a lot of money, and so Tony says to me to go over, keep them company, and see what they're about."

Dehan frowned. "What did he mean, see what they're about?"

"Well, they were Mexican? And they had a lot of money. So this is like Tony's kind of area. It's like it belongs to him. He looks after people, if they have problems they go to him . . ."

Dehan nodded. "He's with the Mob and this is his patch."

"Yeah, I guess you could put it that way."

"And he wanted to know if Fernando was trying to move in."

"I guess."

"So what happened?"

"It was nothing like that. They were just out having a night on the town. And at first Fernando was real nice and cute, and when Tony knew they was okay, he came over and had a drink, and we, you know . . ." She grinned and giggled. "We did a little coke and I said why didn't we go back to their place and have a party, you know, like you do. But Fernando and his friend said no, they wasn't local, why didn't we go to my place? Then two of his pals took off, they had a flight to catch or somethin', and I said, well my place ain't a palace . . ." She gestured around. "You can see! I'm saving for somethin' better, you know? I ain't gonna be in the game all my life."

"That's admirable. What happened?"

"So I says, well, okay, let's invite another chick from the club and go back to my place. But Fernando and this other guy, I can't remember his name, they say no, just me and them." She shrugged. "Well, okay, I'm into that. So we come back here. We do a bit of coke to, you know, get in the mood, like . . ."

Dehan asked, "Who provided the coke, Melanie?"

"They did. They was real generous. They had plenty. Anyhow, I put on some music and start dancing, and I tells Fernando to come and dance with me. Meanwhile his friend is just sitting and watching. So when Fernando gets up to dance with me, I ask him, you know, like, being courteous, what does he want to do with his friend? And then, everything changed."

"Changed how?"

"All of a sudden . . ." She pulled a handkerchief from her pocket, blew her nose, and dabbed her eyes. When she spoke, her voice was nasal and a bit squeaky. "All of a sudden he calls me a whore and a bitch, and slaps me across the face. He hit me so hard I fell down. I asked him what I done, what was wrong, but he just kept hitting me and calling me horrible names. Meanwhile, his pal just sat there and watched. I begged him to stop, begged his friend to make him stop, but he wouldn't. The son of a bitch put me in the hospital and I couldn't work for four months."

I spoke for the first time, and she had to crane around to see me. "Did Tony take care of you?"

"Uh-huh." She turned back to Dehan. "He was real good. He paid my rent, made sure I had food, my medical bills. Everything. He said if I would have called him that night, he would have killed them, but they was out of his juris... jury..."

"Jurisdiction."

"Uh-huh, there was nothing he could do unless they come back."

Dehan asked, "Had you ever seen these men before?"

"Uh-uh, never. And I never seen them since. They know what they's gonna get if they come back. Tony will take care of them. For sure."

Dehan scratched her head and after a moment she said, "Melanie, I know this is horrible for you, but we are nearly done, and this is really helpful for us. After he had beaten you, did Fernando or the other man rape you?"

Melanie looked blank for a moment. "Well, I never thought of it like that till now. I mean, like, they paid, right? But I guess by then I didn't wanna do it, so yeah, I guess in that sense they did."

"Both of them?"

"Uh-huh. First Fernando and then his pal."

"What did his pal look like, Melanie, can you describe him?"

"Mexican, 'bout five-ten, five-eleven. I remember he had real strong hands. Well built, probably in his late forties, curly hair going gray, big Mexican moustache. And he had a funny smell. It was strange, but it was kind'a nice."

"Like paint?"

"Yeah, like paint, and kind of pepper? Jeez, I wish I could remember his name. It didn't sound Mexican, it was more like Russian..."

I said, "Gregor?"

She craned around and shook her head.

"Stephan?"

"Uh-uh."

"Boris?"

"No..."

"Giorgio?"

"That's it!" She snapped her fingers. "It's like Italian? But there's a city in Russia called Georgia, ain't there?"

I nodded. "Yeah, it's actually a country. And also a state in the U.S.A."

"No kidding?"

"Go figure."

I looked at Dehan. She nodded and we stood. "Thanks for your time, Melanie. That's all we needed to know."

"Is that it?" She looked almost disappointed. "You don't wanna, you know... Your birthday an' all?"

I shook my head. "No, Melanie, thanks all the same." At the door I stopped. "What are you going to do when you quit the game?"

She was still sitting on the sofa, watching us leave. "I thought I'd buy a ranch in Texas. Tony says he'll help me out."

I nodded. "You take care, Melanie. Make smart choices."

We let ourselves out and stood a moment, staring at the car. She handed me the keys and went to the passenger door. "Let's get some lunch. I need to eat and think."

I drove back via Market Street to the New Jersey Turnpike, and then headed north. On the way, Dehan spoke.

"I think you're right. This is all about a kind of weird, Freudian relationship. I don't know what your exact idea is, because you won't tell me. Shut up." I shrugged with my eyebrows, but she ignored me and went on. "But here is how I see it.

"I read somewhere, or maybe you told me, that only seven percent of communication is words, right? Which means that ninety-three percent is subliminal, nonverbal. So what does that mean for our case?"

I glanced at her. Her face told me it was a rhetorical question and not to answer it.

"It means," she went on, "that Cyril learned from a very early age to be a victim! And wherever Cyril went, and whatever Cyril did, he was sending out subliminal, nonverbal communication to everybody around him saying, 'Look at me, I am a victim.' He's sitting in the corner, not talking, not participating, looking at his shoes, with his shoulders hunched and his knees together. In nonverbal language he is shouting, 'I am a victim!'"

I nodded. "Interesting."

"Shut up! Now, if ninety-three percent of communication is nonverbal and subliminal, that means that somehow we are tuned, like radios, to pick up those subliminal messages, right? And just as some people have good hearing and others are deaf, some people, like Fernando, are really good at picking up those messages. And the minute he saw Cyril, his radar went crazy and he thought, 'Aha! Here is a victim,' because Fernando, contrary to what we have been told, is a son of a bitch, a bully, and a sadist."

"Strong words, but I agree."

"Now, we need to think, Stone, what was going on, what was the scene, before Cyril showed up at the art classes? We have these two sons of bitches, these two animals, probably using the classes as a hunting ground, where they can select victims to prey on. And into that hunting ground comes Sue Benedict, who fits Fernando's model to a T, if Melanie is anything to go by. So Fernando thinks it will be good sport to bring Cyril into the group, make him fall in love with Sue, and then have Sue fall in love with him or Giorgio, and watch Cyril go to pieces."

"That's an awful lot of assumptions there, Dehan."

"Wait. Now, Fernando sets about his game, constantly pushing Cyril onto Sue, and Sue onto Cyril, sometimes literally, physically, getting her to sit on his lap, or give him hugs, who knows what?

"What he doesn't count on is what we discussed before, that Sue and Cyril actually start becoming friends. Now, here is a question for you: according to both Fernando and Giorgio, Sue was flirting like crazy that night. She was wild, coming on to both Fernando and Giorgio, getting drunk, stoned, the works, right?"

"Right."

"Actually, two questions. One: Isn't that a perfect description of the scene they *paid for* with Melanie?"

I nodded. "Yes indeed, it is."

"Second: If she was so hot and so wild that night, why the hell did she go home at two o'clock? It is a question that has been nagging at me from the beginning. Why the hell did she go home?"

"They both said she had drunk too much. Maybe she overdid it and felt sick."

"That is the obvious answer, but . . ." She held up her thumb. "One, if she was as hot and wild as they described her, she would have had to be very drunk to feel ill enough to leave the party where she was having so much fun, yet the scene Bob Smith described, that he saw through his window outside her apartment, does not fit a woman that drunk. She was coherent, unhappy, angry, but not drunk to the point of feeling ill."

She raised her index finger. "Two, if she was so ill that she needed to leave the party where she was having so much wild, crazy fun, why did she let her visitor in? Why did she even open the door to him? If she was that ill, she should have been either throwing up in the can or comatose in bed. Fernando and Giorgio lied about her state and her behavior, Stone. And if they lied about that, we have to be asking ourselves, not 'why?,' but, what are they trying to hide?"

FOURTEEN

WE HAD COLLECTED A COUPLE OF BEEF SANDWICHES and a couple of coffees from the deli at the end of the road. Now we were sitting at our desks, eating and staring at each other. It was a habit we'd fallen into over the last couple of years. It freaked some people out and annoyed others, but it helped us think. Mo slouched past after a while and muttered, "Jeez, get a room, will ya!" Which made Dehan snigger.

I swallowed and shrugged. "We always come back to the same problem, the forensic evidence does not point to either Giorgio or Fernando." She drew breath and I shook my head. "However clever and thorough your theory is, until we have some concrete evidence, it is just that, a theory."

"So we pull them in, Stone. We separate them and we work on them, play them against each other until one of them breaks."

"Pull them in on what grounds? The only thing we have them on is beating up Melanie, and she already told us she won't testify."

She grunted, sighed, chewed, and stared out at the winter afternoon. Then she wagged a finger at me. "Okay, Sensei, what about the cases in Texas, New Mexico, and Arizona? We go through those files with a fine-tooth comb." She leaned forward with her elbows on the desk and pointed at me. "If we can link the cases, not just to Fernando but to each other, then we can threaten him with handing it over to the Feds."

I nodded and smiled. "That's nice. Tell him to roll on Giorgio or we hand it over to the bureau . . ."

"Exactly, meanwhile we do the same to Giorgio."

"There is something else." I unwrapped my second sandwich and took a bite. "It's been on my mind since the first time we visited Giorgio. He lives way above the means of a private art teacher. His furniture, the house, that's all pretty expensive stuff. Same is true, though less so, of Fernando. Put that together with their visit to Tony's nightclub, the way they were throwing money and coke about, and Tony's refusal to go after them when they beat up one of his girls . . ."

"You're right. That was weird. The Mob are not tolerant of that kind of thing. If they let it pass, there must be a reason."

"The reason is coke. There was coke at the Halloween party and there was coke at Melanie's party. I don't doubt that Giorgio is serious about art and about teaching, but I have no doubt either that he makes his living selling coke and probably weed, and two gets you twenty part of the reason for his classes is to find customers and to distribute. This way he doesn't attract attention and doesn't need to challenge the gangs for a street corner."

She grunted. "I like it. We don't need to charge them. You go get Giorgio, I go get Fernando. We let them see each other being taken into separate interrogation rooms. Then we start to hit them: we've applied for a warrant to see their financial records, we're looking at their phone records to see who they call on a regular basis, we don't need a warrant for that, we know about Texas, New Mexico, Arizona, we are ready to hand the whole damn case over to the Feds if they don't cooperate. Then we play them against each other, tell Giorgio Fernando's cooperating and tell Fernando Giorgio is singing like a bird. If they are even a little guilty, they'll crack."

I nodded. "It's very good, Dehan. It'll work, but before we get started, let me ask you a couple of questions."

"Sure, what?"

"One, why are you convinced it wasn't Cyril?"

She flopped back in her chair and took a deep breath. "I guess," she said after a moment, "his behavior. He had the whole plan set out, to move, leave his job, go to Europe . . . And then when Sue was killed, he just freaked and took his own life. That to me isn't consistent with a man who has killed her, however crazy he is." She paused, thinking. "You know? If he'd killed her in a fit of rage, I could understand the remorse and then suicide. But the careful planning followed by his chaotic behavior, culminating in his suicide. It doesn't wash." She shrugged again. "Also, Stone, his impotence. He *couldn't* have raped her."

I frowned. "But he could have consensual sex with her?"

"I think so. After the visits to Xara, if she was nice to him, I think so." For a moment she looked exasperated. "But even if it *was* him, and I'm pretty sure it wasn't, how would you ever prove it? Unless you go and tear down the East Second Casino Hotel and dig up the foundations, you will never have any forensic evidence."

"Okay, fair point. Now, last question, what if we prove everything we suspect Fernando and Giorgio of, but we can't make Sue's murder stick?"

"It'll stick."

"What if they didn't do it?"

She was shaking her head. "They did, and it will stick. If they didn't, then we'll cross that bridge when we come to it."

I nodded. "Okay."

She watched me a moment. "We on board? You with me?"

"Yeah, sure. Let's go for it."

Half an hour with the files from the Texas, New Mexico, and Arizona cases showed us that they were, indeed, in some respects, linked. They were linked in that they showed a pattern of behavior, and in that they suggested strongly that Fernando

Martinez was involved in the drugs trade. How deeply he was involved was not clear, but each case involved the consumption of cocaine in a brothel where he later went on to beat up a prostitute. What was perhaps more important, however, was that all the prostitutes fit the same general description as Sue Benedict and Melanie. After forty-five minutes, Dehan closed the Texas file and looked at me.

"I'm ready to go. How do you want to do it? You go get Giorgio and I get Fernando? Or we go get one and then get the other?"

I was thinking about it when the internal phone rang. Dehan picked up the receiver, saying to me, "I say we bring Giorgio in first . . ." then, into the phone, "Yeah, Dehan . . ." Her face went rigid. "Okay. We're on our way." She hung up and stood.

"What is it?"

When she answered, it was almost a growl. "Fernando. The son of a bitch just got himself murdered."

I swore quietly under my breath and followed her out, pulling on my coat.

The heavy sky had started to snow thick, slow flakes that were beginning to settle and drift. We made our way across the slippery blacktop to the car at a half run and climbed in. I reversed out carefully and pulled onto Story Avenue, headed west, with the wipers going, spreading the snow across the windshield in a thick sludge. It was not yet five o'clock, but it was already growing dark, and the lights of the slow-moving traffic were a haze through the smeared flakes. I turned onto Soundview and Dehan started to talk.

"It was called in by his downstairs neighbor when he noticed a stain on the ceiling that had started to drip. A patrol car turned up and the uniforms broke into the apartment, found him dead on the living room floor. That's all we have for now."

It was less than half a mile's drive and we got there in a couple of minutes. There were two patrol cars parked outside and the uniforms were putting up tape. I did a U-turn, got some honks from cold, angry drivers, and parked behind one of the patrols. Gunter was at the door.

"Sergeant?"

"Hi, Detective. He's on the top floor. ME and Crime Scene ain't got here yet but they're on the way. It's not nice up there."

"Okay, thanks. Canvass the neighbors, will you? Get statements. Who was watching the house?"

"Detectives Warren and Groves." He pointed to a burgundy Corolla a couple of cars down. "They's parked just down there, in the Toyota."

I followed the direction he was pointing and saw Groves hauling his bulk out of the driver's seat and Warren's head bobbing over the roof on the passenger's side. We crunched through the snow to meet them. Groves was already shaking his bald head and spreading his hands. "I'm sorry, Stone, we was told to watch for him comin' out, not who was goin' in. Either way . . ." He looked back at Warren, tall in a coat that looked too small for him, stamping his feet and billowing clouds of condensation as flakes of snow settled on his mass of curly hair. He said, "Just to pass the time, we made a list of everybody who went in and out. You gotta do somethin' on a night like this, right? And we got tired of playing I spy."

Dehan said, "You guys are the best. You got the list?"

Groves' mouth sagged. "Who are you? And what did you do with Carmen Dehan?" He turned his gape on his partner. "You hear that, Warren? We're the best! Where's the list?"

"Yeah, see, then we got to making paper airplanes . . ."

They both laughed raucously, then Warren handed over a crumpled piece of paper. Dehan took it. Her shoulders were hunched, and her cheeks looked very pink. Warren was saying, "You got quite a bit of coming and going, especially in the last hour. Some people I deduced lived in the block. You know? You see them come in, then a minute later a light comes on, or a drape gets closed, you figure, okay, fat guy with the baseball cap lives on the first floor." He pointed at the list with a gloved finger. "So I made a note, see? Entered three fifteen, drapes closed, yadda yadda. Then the babe comes in at four oh three, four twenty she goes out and comes back at four forty with groceries. She lives here. What apartment? I don't know. So yous can work through the list like that. Can we go home now?"

I nodded. "Nice work. Above and beyond. Thanks."

They both shook their heads and walked away, talking in stage whispers. *"They done something to Stone, and Dehan. It's gotta be body snatchers, or clones..."*

Dehan followed them with a baleful glare. "See? That's why I don't talk to them. Let's go look at the scene."

I climbed the stairs with Dehan just behind me and cold, damp air clinging to my ankles. We reached the top landing and found the door ajar, with yellow tape strung across it. I ducked under the tape and nudged the door open. It was, as Sergeant Gunter had said, not nice.

He was on the floor, lying on his back. His hands were clenched into fists at shoulder height. His eyes were open, staring up at the ceiling, and his mouth was contracted into a horrific grin. He didn't have a lot to grin about. He'd been gutted like a fish, from his pubic bone to his solar plexus, and the wound was sagging open.

Dehan stood beside me and swore softly. Then she said, "His guts. They are all on the inside."

I nodded. "And there isn't much bleeding. Remember the neighbor called it in because there was blood leaking through the ceiling? That's not the wound that killed him. The wound that killed him's in his back. This wound was inflicted once he was lying down. But notice the position of his arms?"

"Yeah, it's like his back went into spasm."

"I'm betting Frank's going to find a stab wound in his back, probably to the heart."

I turned back to the door and examined the lock. There were no scratches, no signs of tampering. Dehan said, "Anything?"

"No."

"So he lets his killer in *and* turns his back on him. He knew him, and he wasn't scared of him."

I returned to the room and took a moment to assimilate the scene. Outside a siren wailed. "The drapes are open, so it was probably still daylight. He's facing the door. What is he? Four, five paces from it? He has one chair over by the window and the sofa on his left, and they are both behind him. He's kind of level with this nearest chair, right?" She nodded. I pointed at a collection of bottles and glasses on a small sideboard on the left, beside the TV. "The drinks are over there. The kitchen is through that door over there." I pointed to a door on the far right. "I guess the bathroom and the bedroom are down there too. So, what's left?" I looked at her. "What's over here? What was he doing? Where was he going? He's standing in the middle of the floor, facing the door. There is nothing over here and his killer is behind him. What's he doing?"

Dehan studied him awhile, visualizing the scene. "Huh," she said at last. "He doesn't look like he was fleeing: he wasn't running." She gave her head a little jerk. "There were two people? He was talking to one of them while the other stabbed him? Or somebody rang at the bell? Pizza?"

"Maybe. That position of his hands, though. It's weird. If he was walking to the door . . ." I made a short walk to demonstrate. "Your hands hang down by your side, don't they? You get stabbed in the back, your shoulder blades contract, but your hands are down. His are up, like a begging dog."

"Two men. He was warding off an attack from the front, and got stuck from behind . . ."

"Hmm . . . maybe."

The tramp of feet on the stairs told us that Frank had arrived with the Crime Scene team. We turned to greet them. Frank nodded at us as they bustled through the door with their equipment, the CS guys in their weird, white plastic suits. There were a couple of subdued, "Detectives," but mostly they just got to work. Frank hunkered down beside Fernando's body and pulled on his latex gloves. A camera started to click and flash. I took a couple of steps nearer, with Dehan beside me. Frank spoke without looking up.

"Don't come any closer. What do you want?"

"His right hand."

"You want his right hand? Carmen, what is wrong with your husband?"

"No." I pointed. "Look at it, the index finger, there is a smear of blood."

He examined it with care for a moment. "There doesn't seem to be a cut. I'll have a closer look back at the lab."

"Could be the killer's DNA."

"You are not only stating the obvious, John, you're interfering with my work. Haven't you got something useful to do? Somewhere else? Come and see me at the lab later and I can give you answers."

I ignored him and stood a moment with my hands imitating Fernando's, pulling in my shoulder blades as though my back had gone into spasm. Then I relaxed my back and watched where my hands went. Dehan was watching me curiously. I turned to her and maneuvered her around so she was standing between me and the door. Then I cupped her cheeks in my hands, like I was about to kiss her.

She raised an eyebrow at me. "Not that this isn't nice, Stone, but a little inappropriate, don't you think?"

"As I kiss you, you stab me in the back."

I heard Frank snort behind me. "The cry of men down the ages."

I leaned in and felt Dehan's fist thump my back, right over my heart. I contracted my shoulder blades and watched my hands wind up in the same position as Fernando's.

Dehan said, "Holy cow."

I turned to look down at him. "He was kissing whoever killed him, and the blood on his hand is from his killer's face."

Frank had stood and was staring at me. "Very ingenious, Stone, but you'll understand that we are not going to turn him over here to inspect his back; not in his present condition. I'll check him when I get him to my lab, and that's where I'll determine cause of death. Though I do tend to agree with you, he was already dead when he was gutted. Let's get him into a body bag." This last was directed at the guys from the meat wagon.

Dehan and I went through the apartment, examined his bedroom, the kitchen, and the bathroom, but found nothing of any interest, and after fifteen minutes, we went back down to the street, where snow was beginning to fall heavily and a slow, steady stream of headlamps was moving along the avenue: people going home. I shoved my hands deep in my pockets. Dehan stood next to me and leaned on my arm, slapping her hands, stamping her feet, and billowing condensation.

"Stone," she said, and looked up into my face, "I think Fernando was kissing Giorgio when he was killed . . ."

FIFTEEN

We sat in the car with the world slowly disappearing behind the wall of snow accumulating on the windshield, looking at Warren's list. It didn't tell us much. Most of the people coming and going were people who lived in the apartments. There were a few women, and two or three men described as possibly Latino, middle-aged, and of medium build, who could have been Giorgio. But with the cold and the snow, everybody was dressed up in coats, hoods, and scarves, which made precise identification almost impossible.

I switched on the wipers. They churned away the snow, and diffuse lights bathed the cab and gave Dehan's face a strange, ghostly luminosity. She was still studying the list but after a moment sighed and dropped it on her lap.

I said, "Santos and Clay were sitting on Giorgio. If he had left the house, they would have seen it and followed."

"If they had seen it. In this weather, it's not so hard to get away unseen over a backyard fence in the dark."

"Don't forget, it was still light when he was killed." I hit the ignition. "Let's go talk to them anyway."

I did a slow U-turn and we started moving south toward

Patterson Avenue. Dehan shrugged and narrowed her eyes in exasperation. "Who else has a motive?"

"What exactly would Giorgio's motive be?"

"You'd just got through telling him you knew about Fernando's taste for beating up women while Giorgio watched. He knows if we start looking into that, Fernando becomes a suspect in Sue's murder, and with the testimony of the hookers he's beaten up, Giorgio becomes an accomplice. He's looking at a potential life sentence if we make Fernando confess."

"Except that we have the apparently insurmountable problem of the DNA. And whatever our theory might be, A, Giorgio doesn't know about it and B, we have zilch evidence to back it up."

"No." She shook her head. "You looked and sounded convincing. You rattled his cage and he panicked. I'm telling you, Stone, they were lovers, and they were involved in some weird-ass sexual relationship where they got their kicks seducing and beating up women. Sue frustrated them because she flirted but would not submit. Her getting close to Cyril was the last straw, and Fernando lost it. Cyril's semen, whether it was planted or the result of having sex, was a godsend to them because it let them off the hook. But it made Cyril panic and ultimately take his own life."

I was quiet for a while. We turned into Patterson. It was dark and still, with the dim light from the streetlamps barely filtering through the bare, black branches of the trees that fringed the road. What light there was reflected a sickly yellow off the drifting snow and the wet strips of blacktop. I sighed as we crawled toward Taylor Avenue.

"Well, whoever killed Fernando seems to have killed any chance we had of getting a confession out of Giorgio, I'll grant you that much. Playing them against each other was the last move we had, unless we get a hit from the blood on Fernando's hand."

I pulled up at the corner, killed the engine, and frowned at her. "It could have been Tony. It could have been a supplier. It could have been a jealous husband—or wife!"

She held my eye. "It could have been Santa Claus with an early delivery, but it wasn't. It was Giorgio."

I smiled. "You know the nicest thing about being absolutely certain of something?"

"I'm absolutely certain you're going to tell me."

"You are that much more likely to get surprises."

"Tee hee. Can we talk to Santos and Clay now?"

We climbed out and heard the whine of a window sliding down across the road. We crunched through the snow and saw Clay looking out at us. "Wa's happenin', Stone, Dehan? Heard your other bird got iced."

Dehan answered. "Do you study that kind of dialogue at hard-ass school?" She turned to me. "His dad's a senator and he graduated from Harvard, you know that, right?" He did some high-pitched wheezing and she asked, "Has there been any movement here? Has he left the house?"

"No, man. We would'a followed him, right? We got visual on the front door and on the backyard. There ain't no way he can git out without bein' seen." He scowled then. "He in there with a nice fire an' a bottle of wine, ain't it? Only a dumbass gonna be out on a night like this."

I smiled. "What does that make us?"

"Four dumbasses. The Dumbass Club."

"I guess you're right. Thanks, Clay."

I was about to walk away when he called me back. "Hey, Stone, he had a woman in there since about five. She come out of the house opposite, couple of doors down." He leered. "She be a better witness than us, I reckon."

"Happen you're right, Clay. Let's find out."

"Yeah, now git outta my window, man. You makin' me cold."

We crunched back across the road to Giorgio's house. The drapes were closed, but I could see light filtering around the edges. We climbed the steps to his porch, and I began to hear music. It sounded like jazz. It could have been Miles. Dehan rang on the bell, then knocked on the wood.

The door opened and Giorgio stood looking at us with a glass of wine in his hand. He had something on his face that wasn't sure if it wanted to be a smile, and one eyebrow arched.

"Detectives. I am wondering, is it against the law to tell a detective he's a pain in the ass?"

"Have you left your house this afternoon, Mr. Gonzalez?"

"In this weather? What for?"

Dehan snapped, "Can you just answer the question, Mr. Gonzalez?"

"No! I have not left the house."

"Is there anybody that can confirm that?"

He laughed. "Sure." He turned his head to look back into the house. "Sandy, honey, have I left the house this afternoon?"

A voice came to us in the negative. He smiled at us like he'd done something real clever and he knew we were going to be mad about it. I studied his face for a moment, trying to decide whether he knew what was coming next.

"Mr. Gonzalez, I have some news which you may find upsetting. Would you like me to give it to you here on the doorstep, or may we come in?"

He sighed and rolled his eyes. "Come on in, Detectives." He walked away from the door, talking over his shoulder. "You like my house so much, why don't I make you up a room so you can move in?"

We stepped into the large, warm living area where the huge fire was burning in the hearth. Sandy Beach was sitting curled up on the sofa, holding a glass of wine, where the flames were reflected in rich orange among the oxblood red. She glanced at me as we came in, looked embarrassed, and turned away. Dehan closed the door and Giorgio went to the fireplace. The mantelpiece was a huge beam of driftwood. He leaned his elbow on it and spread his arms wide. "So, Detective Stone, what is your sad news? I have to tell you, I am a happy soul. It is no easy to make me sad. But give it your best shot." He looked at Sandy and grinned. "Eh, Sandy?"

She didn't answer him but looked at me and then at Dehan, waiting.

Dehan said, "When was the last time you saw Fernando, Giorgio?"

"We are on first-name terms, now, Detective? Or should I call you Carmen?"

"Just answer the goddamn question."

He winked at Sandy and chuckled. "Yesterday. He came over and we had dinner. Then he went home, maybe midnight. Is that okay, Carmen? Is that obedient enough for you? You like men to be obedient, Carmen . . . ?"

"He's dead."

He went very still, narrowed his eyes, frowned. "What?"

"Fernando is dead. He was murdered. Probably this afternoon. Did you kill him?"

The approach wasn't subtle, and it wasn't one I would have chosen right then, but I studied his face carefully. What I thought I saw was incomprehension, but it was hard to be sure. He was a performer. He could have been acting. Sandy had gotten to her feet. Her hands had gone to her mouth and her glass fell and smashed on the wooden floor, spilling the red wine among the jagged shards. "*Fernando?* But that's . . . no . . . That's absurd! Why?"

I ignored her and kept watching Giorgio. He frowned and shook his head, like somebody looking at an equation that doesn't make sense. "Fernando is dead? *Murdered?*"

Dehan almost snarled, "I asked you a question, Giorgio. Quit dodging my questions. Did you kill him?"

"No!" He was looking at her like she was crazy. "Why the hell would I kill Fernando? We were like brothers!"

"Where have you been since we saw you this morning?"

"Here! I told you! With this weather . . . Oh my God . . ."

"Can anyone confirm that?"

Sandy stepped forward. "I can. I'm sorry. I am in shock. I'm not thinking. After you left, I came over . . ." She gave me an apologetic glance. "I wanted to see if Giorgio was all right. We spent some time talking and he kindly asked me to stay for lunch. I've been back and forth a couple of times, but not long enough for him to go any significant distance." She smiled again. "We have spent practically the whole day together."

Giorgio went and sank onto the sofa. He covered his face with his hands and started to sob, strange, long, wailing sobs. I spoke while watching him.

"I'm afraid you can't stay here, Ms. Beach."

"Why in the world not? He needs my support now more than ever. I can't leave him alone."

I turned and frowned at her. "Ms. Beach, you need to snap out of it. Whoever killed Fernando might well come after Giorgio next. And believe me, this is one brutal son of a bitch. If he finds you in the house, he will not hesitate to kill you too. You cannot risk being here."

She went very still, like she was trying to grasp what I was saying, but it wasn't real to her. I went and stood over Giorgio. All the arrogant flamboyance was gone. He was staring up at me with wet, swollen eyes.

"Why . . . ?"

"You tell me. Listen, Giorgio, we are not Vice. We don't give a rat's ass what kind of games you get up to, but you need to understand that Fernando was just stabbed in the heart and gutted like a fish, and the same might happen to you if you don't level with us. Are you trafficking?" I pointed around the house. "You're not affording this on art lessons, right?"

His eyes were staring and his lips kept trembling. "A bit of dope, a bit of coke, but we're not in the big league. We don't owe nobody . . ."

"I'm going to put a couple of cops here for the night." I pointed at him. "Step outside to get the paper off your mat and I will put you away for cocaine trafficking. The closest you'll get to a piece of skirt for the next ten years will be when you get screwed in the showers. Do I make myself clear? Do not step outside your house."

I turned and pointed at Sandy. "You, go home. Do not come near this house again. I am not asking. Come near this house and I will prosecute you for obstruction of justice. Now scram!"

She gathered her dignity about her, gave Giorgio a last, tender look, and made for the door. I turned to Dehan. "Go and get Santos and Clay in here, will you?"

She followed Sandy out. I moved the drape and saw Sandy go to her house and let herself in, and Dehan walk to the car, say something to Clay, and start heading back. Without looking at him, I said, "Sandy seems to care for you. You going to treat her the same way you and Fernando treated Sue?"

He spoke in a wet, swollen voice: "We was just playin' games, man. It wasn't nothin' serious."

I let go the drape and walked over to him. I knew Dehan was a good forty-five seconds away, maybe longer in the snow. It was ample for what I had to do. The backhander caught him on the right side of his head and rocked him. His eyes were staring wide and the pupils were dilated. The open right hand caught him across the ear and knocked him half on his side. I grabbed him by the scruff of his neck and dragged him to his feet till his nose was less than an inch from mine.

"What about Melanie, you piece of shit? What about the girls in New Mexico, Texas, and Arizona? How many others are there who didn't go to the cops? Was that playing too? Was that your sick goddamn game? To beat up on girls who couldn't defend themselves? Was that what you planned for Sue at the party that night? Well I got news for you, pal. I'm going to be having a quiet talk with Tony, about how you beat up his girl and how now you're looking to do a deal and turn state's evidence by giving up your contacts in the Jersey Mob. There are two classes of scum who don't deserve mercy as far as I'm concerned, Giorgio, and they are men who hurt children and men who hurt women. I guess you pulled the short straw, huh?"

I threw him back down on the sofa as the door opened and Dehan came in. She gave me a curious look. "Everything okay?"

"Dandy. Giorgio has promised to cooperate, and to stop answering our questions with stupid questions of his own, isn't that right, Giorgio?"

He swallowed and nodded.

Dehan raised an eyebrow at me. "Good..."

Santos, six feet of solid, athletic muscle, came in making small hops, like a frozen kangaroo. Behind him, Clay, six feet six inches of genial brutality, came in slapping his arms and stamping his feet. I pointed at Giorgio. "This guy is under protective custody. He has confessed to trafficking cocaine and marijuana, and he may be the target of a hit. Sit on him till you hear from me. Don't let anybody near him, or him near anybody. I'll talk to Inspector Newman and have you relieved by morning if we haven't taken him in by then. Any questions?"

Clay said, "Yeah, I got a question."

"What?"

"Get the hell out'a here, man! We got this."

Dehan narrowed her eyes. "That's not a question, Clay."

"*I* know that!"

"Come on." I took Dehan's arm. "We have work to do. Let's go."

We went out into the snow and made our way carefully back to the Jaguar. The sky overhead was black, densely freckled by falling flakes. I wiped the windshield clear with my hand. Then we climbed in. Dehan slammed the door, shutting out the night and the cold, and I turned the key in the ignition to start warming up the car. The engine roared for a moment, then settled to a rumble.

Dehan raised both hands. "Stone, just hold on a second, will you? I am so confused. What the hell is going on? What the hell was that back there? Did you just beat up a suspect? He didn't kill

Fernando. He couldn't have. What the . . ." She hesitated. "What the *fuck* is going on, Stone?"

I gave her a moment to settle. "First of all, of course I didn't beat up a witness. If I had, there would have been a lot more blood and weeping involved. Second, what that was back there was me providing us with an excuse to take Giorgio into custody, partly for his protection and partly so that we could question him. Third . . ." I grinned. "You said you were going to work it out for yourself. Well, my dear Dehan, you know my methods, apply them! Ha!"

She eyed me resentfully. "Jerk!" I moved off carefully, moving back toward Soundview Avenue. "At least tell me where we're going."

"The game is afoot, Watson! We ride to hounds! Tallyho!"

She sighed. "*Jerk!* You are such a jerk sometimes . . ."

SIXTEEN

We crawled along Lafayette to Castle Hill and then joined the procession north on the long, slow, slippery drive toward the Jacobi, stopping and starting at one set of lights after another, with a thousand exhausts turning the freezing air into fog, and the icy sludge on the windshield turning the lights to a multicolored haze. Time crawled, cold and wet.

"Okay, Dehan," I said at last, as we were approaching East Tremont. "I will tell you this. There are a couple of things that you have been overlooking from the very start."

She adjusted her woolen hat and sniffed. "There are?"

Her face said she wasn't happy, but I nodded. "Yes. You developed the idea that Cyril had had consensual sex with Sue, and that Sue had been murdered by Fernando and Giorgio. In doing that you overlooked, and ignored, the fact that Sue *was* actually raped."

She was quiet for a bit, thinking, then said, "We *assumed* she was raped because the sex and the murder were almost simultaneous..."

"No. They weren't *almost* simultaneous, Dehan. They *were* simultaneous. You have been focusing on the semen and the distribution of the semen, but the ME's report said other things, remember? The abrasions around the groin that were consistent with forced intercourse, the bruising and scratches around her legs and hips, and above all the fact that she was being choked. It was all consistent with rape."

"But the only person who was with her was the guy who turned up *after* Fernando. Who we assume was Cyril. She let him in..."

"I'm pretty sure it was Cyril, and I hope we will find out for sure a little later tonight."

"*How?*"

"One thing at a time. Keep going. Let's assume for the sake of the argument that it was Cyril."

I turned right into East Tremont, where the traffic was not so heavy, and we moved at a steady twenty miles per hour toward Silver Street. Dehan sighed.

"Okay, for the sake of the argument. We know from Xara, the hooker that Cyril used to visit, that he could not achieve an erection. So how could he rape Sue without one?"

"But you yourself said that he might be able to with Sue."

"If she was nice and loving to him! But to rape her?"

I sighed and shook my head. "Sex is not an act of love, Dehan. We have discussed this before. It is strictly an act of procreation. It is a very intimate act, so it lends itself to loving feelings, but at its core it is an act of domination and subjugation, where one animal inseminates another."

"Jesus, Stone!"

"Don't get personal, Dehan. This is a murder investigation. We deal in brutal truths. What *we* may bring to the bedroom, or the kitchen table, is our personal business. But murder, rape, and sex are intimately connected at the organic level. You know that."

"I guess..."

"So it follows that violence and domination can be just as sexually arousing as love and affection."

"So you think Cyril raped and murdered Sue? It doesn't make much sense, Stone. What about leaving his job and his house?

Handing in his notice? The trip to Geneva? His suicide? There is a whole pattern of behavior there that is not consistent with his raping and murdering her."

"No. Again, it is not consistent with your view of how and why he would rape and kill her. It's different. You are trying to make Cyril Browne behave like Carmen Dehan. You have to ask yourself, what motivates Cyril Browne?"

She was very quiet while I turned up Silver Street and crossed the Williamsbridge Road. Five minutes later, we were pulling off Seminole Avenue and parking outside the Van Etten Building. She opened the door, and a blast of icy air entered the car and made me shudder. "Okay," she said, "so what motivated Cyril Browne?"

"His mother," I said.

I climbed out and we made our way unsteadily toward the entrance. "But surely," she said, holding on to my arm and trying not to pull me over, "if Sue was like his mother, that would be an overpowering reason *not* to kill her!"

"Things may become a little clearer for both of us in a moment, Dehan."

We found Frank at the autopsy table. On the table was Fernando, looking a little yellow, with small purple patches all over his body. He was facedown now, but I didn't inquire as to how they had stopped his insides from moving outside in the process. What I could see was a large, ugly wound at about the height of his fifth intercostals. It was about one and a half inches long, and the edges had inflamed and curled up like labia. Frank didn't bother with greetings. He pointed at the wound and said, "That's what killed him. He probably used a kitchen knife, judging by the shape of the wound: it is deltoid, slightly wider on one side than the other, two inches long, and about six inches in depth. Probably had it concealed in his sleeve. Interesting thing . . ."

He led us around the table so we could see the left side of

Fernando's neck, and pointed to a purple bruise in the shape of two closed brackets. I said, "A love bite?"

"Mm-hm." He nodded. "The saliva was still wet and abundant, which, given this weather, is hardly surprising. Nothing dries in this. Our house is full of wet washing, even with the dryer. I have sent it off for DNA profiling."

Dehan frowned. "You sent your washing for DNA profiling?"

"The saliva, Carmen. Try to keep up. This killer has either never watched CSI or just doesn't give a damn about being caught."

I glanced at Dehan. "Remind you of anything?"

Frank answered. "Your Sue Benedict case. But the two murders are quite different. The gutting was postmortem, as you had surmised. He bled out quickly and copiously from the wound in his back, which had pierced his heart. With Sue Benedict, the killing was strangulation, from the front, during rape. And the postmortem mutilation was a frenzy of stabbing. Plus, she was obviously killed by a man. This murder, and the postmortem mutilation, were brutal, but cool and calculated, and could well have been committed by a woman. Probably were, I would say."

Dehan scratched her head. "Why?"

"Well, amongst other things, because there are traces of lipstick on his neck, around the love bite. I know in our modern, rainbow society men also wear lipstick, but in my experience, statistically, it is more likely to be worn by a woman."

I asked, "What about the blood on his hand?"

"Not his. Look . . ."

He showed me Fernando's right hand. There were no cuts. But there were bruises on the inside of his index and middle fingers. I nodded. "That's what I thought," I said.

Dehan swore softly. "An earring. He had her face cupped in his hands. She stabbed him in the heart. He went into spasm and tore her earring from her ear."

"Assuming," I said, "and we *are* assuming, that it's a woman.

If there is one thing that defines this case, it is the dark, Freudian sexual undercurrents that move these people."

Frank grunted. "Thankfully not my department."

I rested my ass against one of his benches and folded my arms. "Speaking of departments, what about the stuff I left with you?"

"Things are a lot quicker these days, thanks to the Panasonic-IMEC developments, but we still can't perform miracles. I have the results on some of it."

Dehan was frowning, looking from Frank to me and back again. "What stuff?"

Frank said, "The thread."

"What thread?"

I smiled. "Remember the splinter I had in Elk Grove?"

"Yeah, what was that?"

"I saw the needle had been threaded, but she hadn't started embroidering with it yet. So the tail end of the thread was still there. What do you do just before you thread a needle?"

"Nothing. I never sew."

"What did your mother do, just before she threaded a needle?"

Her face lit up. "You *are* smart, Stone! She would suck the thread to make a point, so it would go through the eye."

"Exactly, and then tie it in a little knot. I asked if I could have it. She agreed, and so I lawfully removed a sample of her DNA. What was the result, Frank?"

"I have it in my office. I'll send it to you later by email, but I can tell you that there is a very close family relationship, such as brother and sister, between Mary Browne and the man who raped and murdered Sue Benedict. He was her brother." He shrugged. "If Cyril was her only brother, then Cyril killed Sue Benedict."

"Holy cow, Stone!" Dehan stared at me with wide eyes. "So that's it, you solved the case . . ."

I shook my head. "Not quite. There are a lot of loose ends to be tidied up. Like why Fernando was murdered, and by whom. We are not there yet."

"Well, he clearly wasn't murdered by Cyril. You figure a woman, Frank?"

"In all probability. In all my years doing this job, I have never seen a man stab to the heart, in the back, in an embrace. Typically, men will stab low to the gut or the solar plexus, up under the rib cage. Even in an embrace. Women kill a lot less than men, and they are typically devious when they do, because usually they are aware that their intended victim, if he is a man, is physically stronger than they are. I have never seen a man kill like this."

Dehan shrugged. "A woman with a motive for stabbing Fernando in the heart. Hum, let me see." She puffed out her cheeks and blew. "Let's face it, that's not a small pool of suspects, but chances are we're going to get a hit on CODIS because, as you would say, Stone, two gets you twenty she's one of the hookers he's beaten up."

I nodded. "That would be the obvious explanation."

"Don't complicate this, Stone." She grinned and wagged a finger at me. "*Entia non sunt multiplicanda praeter necesitatem.*"

Frank went rigid and stared at her. "What have you done to her, Stone? She's broken."

I laughed. "It's Occam's razor in the original Latin. She does it to annoy."

"It means," she said, "things should not be multiplied beyond what is necessary. In other words, don't complicate things."

"That is true," I said. "And William of Occam was a very wise man indeed. But are you sure you are looking at the simplest answer? Are you sure you are not complicating things unnecessarily?"

She crossed her arms. "Okay, genius, what's your theory?"

"I must say," put in Frank, "I am pretty curious to hear it myself. If this man beats up women for fun, it's a cinch one of those women killed him."

I shook my head. "Uh-uh, I plan to wait for the DNA results and then say, 'See? I knew it!'"

Frank sighed. "I always said he was a fraud. Now please get

out. I have places to be and people to dissect. I shall call you when I get the results."

We left him to his dissecting and made our way out. In the lobby I stopped, called the station, and asked to be put through to Clay. It rang a couple of times and a deep voice said, "I *told* you we got this, mother hen," then laughed. "What do you *want*, Stone?"

"I believe you. Has he said anything?"

"Like what?"

"Like any kind of confession?"

"Nah, he just regalin' us with wild stories of wild parties, cocaine and crazy chicks. I missed my vocation, man. I gonna hand in my badge and become a cocaine-traffickin' artist."

"I'm sure you'll prosper. Anyone call, visit, ring at the door . . . ?"

"No."

"Okay, we're on our way to the station. I'll talk to the inspector and . . ." I thought for a moment. "Yeah, what the hell, we'll bring him in."

"Ten four, man. We'll be waitin' for your call."

I hung up and Dehan said, "Bring him in for what?"

I didn't answer straightaway. Finally I gave my head a small twitch and said, "Drug trafficking, at the very least."

I took the chains out of the trunk and put them on the wheels. The snow was getting deep on the roads. There were barely any pedestrians, and the traffic had thinned out to the odd, sporadic vehicle crawling through the gossamer veils of falling flakes.

It took us a good forty minutes to get to the station, and by the time we had collected two cups of coffee and climbed the stairs to the inspector's office, we were cold, tired, and pretty miserable. His office was warm and he was, as always, welcoming.

"What an appalling night to be out solving murders! Tell me, I have been going over the original report and I am intrigued, how are you getting on? How is it going? Sit! Sit!"

Dehan sat in an armchair, clutching her cup with both hands, and I sat in the chair across from him at his desk. I was still thinking about my answer to his question when Dehan started to talk.

"Stone managed to get a DNA sample from Mary Browne."

"Oh!" His eyebrows shot up. "I thought she was set against that."

"She was, but she gave him a needle with a piece of cotton attached . . . It's a long story, sir. In any case, the man who killed Sue Benedict was Mary Browne's brother."

"Splendid work, Stone! So now we just have to find him."

"No, we found him, sir. He is now an integral part of the foundations of the East Second Street Casino Hotel, in Reno."

"Good Lord!"

"He committed suicide by throwing himself into the wet concrete."

"Well . . ." He looked from me to Dehan and back again. "Case closed, then. What about this Fernando Martinez character?"

"He and Giorgio Gonzalez have been involved in small-scale coke and marijuana trafficking for a few years. They also got their kicks by beating up and raping women, mainly hookers, we think, but not exclusively. We think they used the art classes both as an outlet for their merchandise, and as a hunting ground for girls. And it was in that environment that Cyril met Sue. It may have precipitated the killing, through jealousy or something of that sort. We just don't know. The night she was killed, they were all at a party together. With the alcohol and drugs going down, it is hard to form a clear picture of the events."

"Yes, I see. The Halloween party." He thought for a moment. "So is it your opinion that Fernando Martinez's death is related to the original case? Or simply a bizarre coincidence?"

She glanced at me. "I'm not exactly sure of Stone's views on that, sir, we are still thinking it through. It seems he was stabbed in the back, with a kitchen knife, while he was kissing a woman.

My own opinion is that he was probably murdered by one of the women he abused."

"Yes, I see. That seems to make sense."

"We thought at first that Giorgio Gonzalez, Sue Benedict's art teacher, might be involved, but he has a pretty airtight alibi. He had spent practically the whole day with his neighbor."

The inspector turned and frowned at me. "You are uncharacteristically quiet today, John. Usually it is you doing all the talking, while Carmen here observes a discreet silence. Are you going to share your thoughts with us? What do you plan to do with Giorgio Gonzalez?"

"I'd like to arrest him and bring him in for interrogation, sir."

"Arrest him? On what charge?"

"Trafficking drugs, rape, assault."

"Have you any evidence for these charges?"

"He confessed to trafficking cannabis and cocaine in front of me and Dehan, sir. We also have the testimony of Melanie in Jersey. Now that Fernando is dead, she may be willing to testify in court. The truth is, sir, any charge will do. I just want him in custody because I think his life is at risk. In fact, the more I sit here and think about it, the more convinced I am that we are on the clock. Somebody is going to try and kill him, somebody very subtle and very dangerous. He is with Santos and Clay right now, but I would feel a lot more comfortable if we had him safely behind bars, for his sake."

He had listened to me with a deep frown on his brow. Now he turned to Dehan. "Do you agree with this assessment, Carmen? Did you hear Gonzalez confess to trafficking?"

"Yes, sir, I did. And Stone has been right about this whole damn case all along, so if he says Giorgio is at risk, I am willing to believe that."

"Fine, that is good enough for me." He nodded and turned to me. "Bring him in, John."

I pulled my phone from my pocket and called Clay again. A voice came on telling me it had not been possible to connect my call. I suppressed a jolt of panic, hung up, and called again. Again the voice, "It has not been possible . . ." I called Dispatch and had them put me through to Santos. It rang three times and was answered.

"Santos, what the hell is going on? Why isn't Clay answering his phone?"

There was silence, with only the slightest sound of breathing. I said, "Santos . . . ?"

A sigh, and then the line went dead. I stood. "*Jesus Christ!*" I wrenched open the door, shouting at the inspector. "Get every available car down there now! Clay and Santos are down! *Do it now!*"

SEVENTEEN

I FORCED MYSELF TO STAY AT THIRTY MILES AN HOUR. I knew that if I went any faster, I'd start fishtailing, skidding, and sliding all over the road and we'd end up taking twice as long. As it was, we fishtailed into Patterson Avenue and wound up with the trunk on the sidewalk and the back wheels spinning in the drift. Dehan took the wheel and I pushed and we finally got it back on the road again.

By the time we arrived at Giorgio's house, the place was like an anthill, only with cops instead of ants. There were five cars there, their red-and-blue lights pulsing ghostly on the snow. The door was open and yellow light was spilling out onto the porch. The uniforms were putting up yellow tape, cordoning off the area. Across the road, I could see Sandy Beach staring out at us through her window. We ducked under the tape and went up the steps to the door. Dehan was just ahead of me. Sergeant Gunter was standing outside.

"Detectives, the ME and Crime Scene are on their way. So is the inspector. Clay is just here . . ."

He pointed through the door. I felt a jolt of adrenaline. The way he said it sounded like he was alive. But when I looked through the door, I saw him lying on his back. He looked surprised to see the ceiling up there. He had a neat hole right in the center of his forehead.

"Gunter, have you started canvassing the neighbors yet?"

"We just got here, Detective, a few minutes before you did. All we've done is secure the scene. We found the door open and the scene exactly as you see it."

"Across the road, two doors down, there's a woman staring out of her window watching. Her name is Sandy Beach. Go get her and bring her here, will you?"

"Sandy Beach? Sure."

He left, and I heard Dehan's voice across the large, hollow room.

"Santos is here..."

I looked over at the sofa and only then became aware that the television was on, playing a rerun of *Castle*. Santos had been watching that, or something else earlier. He was sitting slumped over the arm of the couch. There was a mug of coffee spilled on the carpet, dangling from his fingers. His position was twisted and uncomfortable.

Dehan turned to look at me. "I really want to read this as Giorgio killed them and got away. But that's not what happened here." She pointed at the door. "Somebody knocked or rang. Clay opened and instantly got plugged in the head." She gestured at Santos. "He turned to see what was going on. It must have been a bare second. His piece is still in his holster. Then the shooter stepped in and got him from the door. He must have shot Clay, taken just one step, aimed, and shot Santos. Bam, bam."

I nodded. That was how I had read it too. "So where is Giorgio?"

"Captured or rescued."

I moved over to the sofa. The shot had entered his forehead close to his left temple and blown a big hole in the back of his head. There was a mass of gore and blood over the cushions. I hunkered down and had a look. The slug was clearly visible.

"Nine-millimeter." I stood. "What? Thirty foot? It's a good shot."

She nodded once. "That's what I was thinking. Most people in a hurry would have gone for the body. He's sitting sideways on, twisted around, and the shooter steps in and aims before Santos can react. But he goes for a head shot. That's a lot of confidence. And accuracy at thirty paces."

"The door was left open. The fire has burned down and the room is cold, but the blood is beginning to dry. This happened a while ago. It must have been very shortly after we left."

"The killer was waiting?"

Before I could answer, there was a footfall outside. Then a gasp and a small scream. I moved to the door. Gunter was with Sandy. He looked embarrassed. She had her hands over her mouth and was staring wide-eyed at Clay on the floor. Then she screwed them up and turned away. We stepped out after her, and Dehan put her arm around her shoulders, led her from the door. Gunter looked apologetic. "You told me to bring her over. I warned her it wasn't pretty..."

I patted his shoulder. "Don't worry. My bad."

I followed them down the steps to where they were standing in front of the garage. Sandy watched me approach. I noticed she was wearing her hair caught up at the back of her head. She still had staring eyes, and her hands over her mouth. I said, "I'm sorry you had to see that, Ms. Beach. We've only just arrived and we're still in a bit of turmoil. That was one of our officers."

She slowly dropped her hands. "I'm sorry. I should have been prepared. Your sergeant warned me."

"You're never really prepared, Ms. Beach. I wanted to ask you if you had seen or heard anything."

She gave small, slightly breathless nods. "It was a little after you..." She hesitated.

"After we'd left?"

"Well... yes, after you'd left. I had seen Detective Dehan go to that car and come back in with two men. I was so worried for

Giorgio. I know you warned me to stay away, but I am really very attached to him." She gave a small laugh. "I don't want you to think that I spend my whole life at the window watching for him, but I heard you leave..."

She faltered, and Dehan smiled. "You wanted to see if the two men had left with us, so you could go back to Giorgio again."

Sandy nodded. "I'm afraid so. But I saw that their car was still there. Then I saw another car arrive."

"Can you describe it?"

"It was big, dark blue. It was like the car Gibbs drives."

Dehan frowned. "Gibbs?"

"You know, in *NCIS*."

I said, "A Dodge Charger. So what happened next, Ms. Beach?"

"Two men got out. They were wearing suits—it was hard to tell, but they looked expensive—and dark coats. They were well dressed. They went up to the house, and a short while later, they came out again with Giorgio."

I thought about it a moment, then asked her, "Where did Giorgio sit?"

She was momentarily taken aback. "Oh, well, um, in fact, he sat in the front passenger seat. Is that important?"

Dehan smiled again and shook her head. "Probably not," she said, but we both knew it was a given: if the Mob take you for a ride and sit you in the front seat, you're not coming back. I figured Dehan wanted to spare Sandy that, at least for now.

Sandy took hold of her hands. "Is he all right? Is he going to be okay? They won't hurt him, will they?"

I answered instead of Dehan. "That's what we are trying to find out, Sandy. Why didn't you call me when these men arrived?"

"Well, I had no reason to. They looked so smart, I assumed they were from the police or the FBI or something. I thought they were taking him away to question him."

She had started shivering. Dehan put her arm around her

again and said, "Come on. We'd better get you inside. Is there anyone I can call to come and be with you?"

She shook her head. "That person was Giorgio. Just please bring him back safe and sound."

I watched them cross the road together, picking their way with care.

The sound of a siren preceded an ambulance, the ME's car, and the crime scene van. I called Dispatch and put out a BOLO on a dark blue Dodge Charger driven by two men in expensive suits, and Giorgio Gonzalez, while the fleet of vehicles parked noisily out front. Then people began to spill from their vehicles and doors slammed and echoed in the street, like a firefight.

While the crime scene team suited up and the gurneys were wheeled into the house, Frank approached me, hunched into his shoulders and breathing clouds of vapor.

"What is this, some kind of killing spree?"

"Could be. You got any news for me?"

"If you'd give me a chance to work instead of finding bodies all over the place . . ."

"These two are detectives from the precinct."

"I heard. Look, John, I did get one of the samples done. Don't think I'm going to make a habit of this, but I knew it was important . . ."

I heard a street door slam and looked back over my shoulder. Dehan, with her woolen hat pulled down on her head, was crunching her way back through the snow. As she approached, Frank started talking again. "You're not going to be happy. I said Fernando was probably kissing a woman when he was killed . . ."

Dehan said, "He wasn't? Stone, maybe Giorgio's alibi was a fake. Sandy would do anything for that guy." She looked back at Frank. "It was Giorgio, wasn't it?"

He sighed. "No, listen to me, Carmen. Yes, Fernando was kissing a man. In fact, he was getting a love bite from a man. But the man was . . ."

He hesitated. I supplied the words. "The man was Cyril Browne."

He nodded. "Yes. Almost certainly. Whoever raped and killed Sue Benedict also killed Fernando Martinez."

Dehan turned and walked away, staring around her like she'd lost her mind and was trying to find it. Then she came back and stared at Frank. "*What?* Cyril Browne is *dead*! He jumped into the foundations of the damned Second Street Casino Hotel! *He was seen doing it!*"

Frank shrugged. "Then it's his identical twin. I don't know what to tell you, Carmen. The sample was not contaminated. I double-checked. I also checked to see if Fernando was gay."

"What? How?"

"There are ways. You examine the . . ."

"Yeah, okay, I get it. And?"

"He was either gay or bisexual. He had certainly had anal sex recently."

"So you are telling me that Cyril Browne raped and murdered Sue Benedict, and then had sex with and killed Fernando Martinez."

"Or somebody with an identical DNA profile. That is certainly what the forensic evidence indicates. I had better get inside and look at these bodies."

He walked away and climbed the steps toward the door. Dehan stared me in the face. She was too shocked to be mad. "And you knew." I nodded. She shook her head, then shrugged, screwing up her eyes. "*How?*"

"We have a much more immediate problem, Dehan. Where is Giorgio?"

"Two men in dark suits and a Dodge Charger took him."

"Somebody who was waiting for us to leave."

"And somebody who is skilled and experienced with a gun . . ."

"Who is very cold and very ruthless. Who does that suggest to you?"

TRICK OR TREAT | 151

She puffed out her cheeks and blew a long stream of dense vapor out into the dark. "Well, *not* Cyril Browne, for a start!" She sighed again and gathered her thoughts. "Okay, a Dodge Charger, two men in suits, efficient killers . . . sure! It could be the Mob. Tony."

"For what purpose?"

"We don't know. That's just the thing, Stone. We don't know. We don't know a goddamn thing."

"Keep it together, Dehan."

"Is this even the same case? Is Cyril dead? He has a *twin* now?" She stretched out her arm toward California. "Not in the photos! Not in the articles! Not according to Father Cohen! What is he? A long-lost twin come back from the goddamn Amazon? What? Are we in Dynasty land now? In some damn Mexican soap?"

She thrust her hands in her pockets and stood bending her knees and bouncing, staring across the road. After a while, she said, "Sorry."

"Forget it. I understand."

Another siren sounded in the freezing night and a patrol car turned in from Patterson Avenue and pulled up. The inspector climbed out and approached, clapping his gloved hands. Before he could speak, I said, "Clay and Santos are both dead. Shot in the head with a nine-millimeter. Dehan will fill you in, sir. I need to make a phone call."

I took a walk down the road and phoned my friend Bernie at the bureau.

"Stone. How's married life? You still owe me those beers. I have the tally right here. It stands at three thousand, five hundred and sixty-four."

"Make it sixty-five. I need an urgent favor. I could go through the PD, but you guys are faster because you cheat."

"That's true. It's the only way to get things done."

I told him what I wanted; he told me he'd call me back in five minutes and hung up. I was on the corner of Taylor and Patterson, looking west down the dark, snowing tunnel of the street, with the ineffectual light of the streetlamps obscured by the twisted black branches of the plane trees. At the end of the tunnel, there was only more darkness, but I knew it was Soundview Park, and the freezing, inky Bronx River.

I made my way back toward Giorgio's house with my toes going numb. Dehan was walking to meet me, and behind her I could see the inspector talking on the telephone. As we came together, Dehan said, "He's organizing a manhunt. Every car in the city, choppers, I think he's even getting dogs out to search Soundview Park."

I listened to her, then said, "He's dead."

"What?"

"Giorgio. He's dead."

"How do you know?"

"I don't. I might be wrong. But, you know, I'm not. It's logical. But we need to find him before..."

She was frowning like I was crazy. "Before what, Stone?"

I stood chewing my lip. I stared at her face for a moment, seeing only the movies playing out in my mind. I said, "The logical place would be where the party was. Come..."

I half ran, trying not to slip and fall, up the stairs and into his house, calling to every available uniform to follow me: "I want you to tear this house apart. Check every room, every cupboard, every wardrobe. Check the attic and the cellar if there is one. You and you, check the garage, check the trunk of his car. Check for hollow walls and loose floorboards. There might be a body hidden in this house. If there is, find it!"

It took two hours. Eventually they brought in a dog. We checked every corner of the building, every nook and every cranny. We even knocked on the nooks and crannies to see if they were hollow. Giorgio Gonzalez was not in the house where the Halloween party had been. That house was empty.

Finally the officers and the dog departed to join the citywide search for the Charger. The house was locked up, and the inspector went home, advising us we should do the same. He climbed in the patrol car, the door clunked, and the driver pulled away. As they carefully negotiated the corner, we could hear the choppers over Soundview Park describing their grid-pattern search, growing louder, then dimmer, with their powerful spots trained on the dark, desolate, frozen ground below. They would be using heat sensors too. But they would be useless in finding a corpse, especially in this weather.

In any case, the corpse would not be in the park. That would not make any sense. Everything this killer did had a meaning. And the only thing that made sense—that had meaning—was for the corpse to be where the Halloween party had been.

But it wasn't there.

EIGHTEEN

Dehan took my arm in both of hers. "C'mon, Stone. There's nothing more we can do tonight. Let's go get some rest. I could use a fire, a meal, and a drink."

I looked down into her face. Her brown, woolen hat was pulled low, almost to her eyes, and her nose was red from the cold. "A fire, a meal, and a drink," I said.

"Yeah." She narrowed her eyes and gave me a thin smile.

I said, "Home."

"Mm-hm..."

I walked back to the corner of Patterson and Taylor. This time I didn't look west. I looked across at Bob Smith's house. I could see slivers of light shining through the edges of his drapes. I turned and looked then at the building where Sue Benedict had had her apartment, with the flight of ten steps running up the outside to her front door. All the windows were dark. Dehan came up beside me. "What is it?"

"I'm not sure. Come."

I crossed the road to Bob's house and rang on the bell. After a couple of minutes, he opened the door and smiled at us. He still looked amiably comfortable. "Good heavens!" he said. "You look frozen. Come in, for goodness' sake! Come in and warm up."

We followed him through to his living room, where three cats lay in front of a blazing fire, and a fourth lay across the back of his sofa. "Can I offer you a drink to warm you up?"

I shook my head. "We won't keep you, Mr. Smith. I just have a couple of small questions. The house opposite, where Sue used to live..."

"Yes, on the corner."

"Do you happen to know who lives there now?"

He raised his eyebrows. "No. In fact, I don't think anybody lives there. I can't remember the last person I saw coming in or out. It must be..." He gazed down at the flames, shaking his head slightly. "Oh, at least eight or nine years."

"Did you notice anybody going in or out today?"

He gave his comfortable chuckle. "We haven't been in the garden today, with this weather. So no, I haven't noticed the goings-on in the street, except all the sirens in the last few hours, of course."

I pulled out my phone, dialed, and waited. It rang once and Bernie said, "Stone, I'm not quite ready."

"No, it's something else. I know you have a family, Bernie, but this is critical."

"No problem. She wants a divorce anyway."

I gave him the address. "Who owns this? Also, when Cyril Browne died"—I gave him the details—"who was the beneficiary of his life insurance?"

"This might take a little longer. I'll get back to you."

"Thanks."

I hung up and called the inspector.

"Stone! Any news?"

"In five minutes. Right now I need a search warrant for Sue Benedict's apartment."

"On what grounds, Stone?"

"On the grounds that Giorgio Gonzalez's body is in there."

"How can you possibly know that?"

"Because, if I am right, nine years ago, Mary Browne bought

Sue Benedict's house with the money she got from the insurance payout from Cyril's death."

"Are you sure about all of this, John?"

"I wouldn't be calling if I wasn't sure, sir. Start drafting, I'll confirm it in five minutes."

I hung up and the phone rang. As I answered, I saw Bob coming in from the kitchen with three mugs of black coffee on a tray. I said, "Bernie."

Bob put his finger to his lips and laced each mug with whiskey and winked at Dehan. She grinned and handed me a mug. Bernie was saying, "Yes to your first question."

"Both parts?"

"Yeah, both parts. Outstanding. As regards ownership of the property. It was bought nine years ago by one Mary Browne of Elk Grove, Sacramento, and she is still the sole owner of the property. As to the insurance, she was also the beneficiary of her brother's life insurance. Three-quarters of a million dollars."

"Bernie, can you email these documents to Deputy Inspector John Newman, at the Forty-Third?"

"Sure. That's three more beers you owe me."

"You got it, Bernie."

"Them."

"Yeah, them."

I hung up, took a long pull of the coffee, smacked my lips, and said, "You have to tell me your blend." Then I called the inspector.

"John, what news?"

"My suspicions were right. Confirmation should be arriving in your email now. Sir, I feel the circumstances constitute probable cause. Have I got your permission to pick the lock? I think a man might be dying in there."

He hesitated. "No, John. We'll have a warrant within twenty minutes. Just hold your horses a little longer."

I sighed. "Yes, sir."

I hung up and we all three stood in awkward silence, sipping

Bob's excellent laced coffee. After a moment, Bob frowned. Dehan said, "What is it, Bob?"

He cocked his head. "Did you hear that?"

"No..."

I said, "I thought I did, but it may have been the wind."

He went to his front door and opened it. We all stepped out onto his front lawn. There was no sound but the occasional gusting of the wind and the desultory creak of a branch loaded down with snow.

"There!" he said. "There it was again! Did you hear it? I swear it came from Sue's house. It was like a muffled cry for help. There! There it was again!"

I sighed. "You start to enjoy your coffee and something always crops up. We'd better go and have a look, Dehan. Thanks for the coffee, Mr. Smith."

"Bob." He winked at me. "You're with the Forty-Third. I was forty years with the Forty-Fifth. Go get your man."

We crossed the road back to the corner and climbed the steps to her front door. I pulled out my Swiss Army knife, but Dehan shook her head and muttered, "Put it away, Sensei, you'll only embarrass yourself."

She slid in front of me, pulled something out of her pocket, fiddled for a moment at the lock, and the door opened.

"What did you do?"

"Mean Streets College, Sensei, mean streets."

We stepped inside the dark hall. Pallid streetlight leaned in, making dull stencils of the banisters on the floor and against the walls. I pulled my flashlight from my inside pocket, switched it on, and played it around the small, cramped space. There was a narrow staircase rising to a second floor. On the right there was a door. I opened it onto a room that was pitch black. I said, "You think the lights work?" I reached in and flipped the switch. The lights came on.

The drapes on the right were drawn closed across the windows. The furniture was basic and could well have been fifteen or twenty years old. There was no TV. There were no books, ornaments, or photographs. But the place was clean. There was a white vinyl sofa with matching chairs, a coffee table on a rug.

Dehan moved across the room to the kitchen, separated from the living space by a breakfast bar. She ran her finger over the surface. "Dusted," she said, and opened the fridge. The light inside came on and it started to hum.

"Milk, butter, hummus, eggs. Somebody either lives here or spends time here, Stone."

"Somebody who doesn't watch TV, and hasn't much they want to remember, by the looks of it. You think maybe they're sleeping upstairs?"

I switched on the landing light and climbed the steps without being too careful about making a noise. The landing was small. There was a small bathroom with a shower cubicle. There was soap, unused, but no toothpaste and no toothbrush. The bedroom door was slightly ajar. Inside, it was very dark. There was no snoring, no sound of heavy, sleepy breathing. There was only silence. I went over and pushed it all the way open. Then I switched on the light.

He was on the bed, as I had expected. But what I hadn't expected was to find him handcuffed to the headboard. His ankles were also cuffed to the footboard, so that he was spread out in a big X. His eyes were wide with terror and he was staring at me. But he wasn't seeing me, because he was very dead.

Cause of death was not hard to establish. The duvet between his legs was saturated with blood, which had sprayed as far as the footboard and even spattered the far wall of the bedroom. His genitals had been removed, apparently with a single, clean cut, and placed on his belly. From the gray, pasty color of his face and his naked body, it looked as though he had been pretty much exsanguinated from that single wound.

There were other wounds: savage wounds all over his body. There were multiple stab wounds to his left chest, slashes to his face and his legs, to his torso, his neck, and his arms. But none of these had bled. He had been castrated and allowed to die, and then he had been attacked.

Dehan said, "I'll call Dispatch."

A huge wave of weariness washed over me. I pulled my phone once again from my pocket and called the inspector.

"Stone, I am on it. Just give me . . ."

"Sir, you are not going to believe this."

"What?"

"We have found Giorgio Gonzalez. He's dead. He was castrated and left to bleed to death. After that, he was badly mutilated."

"Poor bastard."

"Agreed on both counts, sir."

"Where was he? You went to the house, didn't you?"

"The neighbor, a cop from the Forty-Fifth, Bob Smith . . ."

"Bob? Sure! I know Bob! He lives there? Whadd'ya know! Damn good cop."

"Yes, sir. He thought he heard shouting from the house, so we thought it best to investigate."

He grunted. "Very well, just as long as we're covered. Are we any closer, John, to knowing who did this?"

"Yes, sir. As I said earlier, I had no doubt as to who had done it. Cyril Browne did it."

"But I thought Cyril Browne was dead!"

"Yes, sir. He is. I'll explain in the debriefing. It's a little bit complicated. But I hope to have an arrest soon."

"Good. We have had quite enough homicides for one night, John."

"Yes, sir. I agree."

I hung up and Dehan and I made our way down to the ground floor. I opened the door and stepped out into the cold. Dehan came close beside me. "You okay?"

I nodded. "It was a difficult call. If I had played it differently, Clay, Santos, and Giorgio might still be alive."

She shook her head. "You can't do that, Stone. You did what seemed right at the time."

"I should have brought Giorgio in straightaway. I didn't see this coming."

"Nobody could have."

"I liked Clay." I smiled. "He was a pain in the ass, but I liked him."

Far off, on Soundview Avenue, the first siren wailed, returning to Patterson Avenue once again. It would soon be followed by others. Dehan slipped her arms around me and we waited there, on the steps, for the patrol cars to arrive.

They came within a couple of minutes, accompanied by Frank and the crime scene team. We went down the steps to meet them. Frank looked pissed. "What the hell is going on, John? We hadn't even got halfway back!"

I tried to smile but failed. "I think I'm done for tonight. At least I hope I am. Upstairs in the bedroom. Giorgio Gonzalez, castrated, bled to death. I have to notify his lover. After that, I am going home."

Frank was frowning at me. "Are you okay?"

"Just tired. Catch you later, Frank. If I'm significantly wrong about cause of death, call me, will you?"

"You won't be."

"See ya."

I put my arm around Dehan, and we walked slowly up Taylor Avenue to Sandy Beach's house. I let go of Dehan and rang the bell. Dehan took my hand and muttered, "Poor woman. She's going to be devastated."

She opened the door almost immediately, smiled brightly, and then frowned.

"My goodness! You look exhausted. Please do come in out of the cold. What can I do for you?"

We stepped inside and she closed the door behind us. The living room and the dining room were on our right, and a passage ran down to the kitchen at the back of the house. On the left, a staircase climbed to the upper floor. She indicated the door to the living room and we went through. Four lamps gave a warm, amber light. There was a fire burning in the grate, and Debussy was playing softly in the background.

"Do sit and get warm. Are you off duty yet? Can I offer you a drink?"

I smiled and sat in an armchair. Dehan sat next to me on the sofa. I said, "Not quite yet, but almost. Ms. Beach, I think you ought to sit down. We have some very bad news."

She went very still. After a moment, she sat in the other armchair. "Is it Giorgio?"

I nodded. "Yes. He's dead, Ms. Beach. I am very sorry."

Her whole body seemed to jolt three times, like the shock was hitting her in stages. Then her bottom lip started to quiver. Tears welled in her eyes and spilled down her cheeks. She clamped her hands to her mouth and gave a small, strangled scream. Dehan rose, pulling a handkerchief from her pocket, and went to sit on the arm of Sandy's chair. She put her arm around her and gave her the handkerchief.

But Sandy fell back, stifling her screams behind her hands, calling on some unnamed divinity to make it not true, to make it so that it was somebody else, not Giorgio.

All we could do was watch her and listen to her grief, and wait for the storm to pass. There was nobody to help her through it. The only person on Earth she had to turn to in moments like these was the one whose death she was grieving. Eventually her convulsive crying began to subside, and her breathing became more quiet. Dehan stood and went to the kitchen. Sandy sat up, blew her nose, and wiped her eyes. We sat in silence until Dehan returned with a glass of water. She gave it to Sandy, who drank half and let out a shaky sigh.

Dehan sat on the sofa again.

I said, "Ms. Beach, Sandy, I am so sorry for the pain you are going through, but I have a couple of questions I need to ask you. Do you feel up to answering them?"

She nodded a couple of times. "I'm sorry. Of course. I'll do my best."

"The first seems a stupid question." I hesitated a moment. "But, how did you know that the Dodge Charger, the one the two men arrived in, how did you know it was blue?"

She stared at me for a long moment, blinking and frowning by turns. "Well," she said, "I saw it."

"Yeah, but you see, I put it to the test out there, and at that distance, in this light, even outside, you can't tell if a car is dark blue or black or even gray."

"My goodness. Well, I suppose I assumed it was blue because that's the color Gibbs' car is on *NCIS*."

I smiled. "Of course, that must have been it. The other question I have is a little more complicated." She was frowning uncertainly at me, as was Dehan.

I said, "How long have you known Mary Browne?"

NINETEEN

She sank back in her chair. Her face had gone very pale.

"What makes you think I know anyone called Mary Browne?"

"Do you?"

"It's an extremely common name."

"Not the way she spells it." She didn't answer, so I pressed her. "Are you telling me, Sandy, that if I get a court order to search your computer, I won't find any emails from Mary?"

She closed her eyes and sighed. "I must say, your timing, Detective . . . I have known Mary for many years, more than I can remember. Since we were small children."

"She bought the house on the corner."

"Yes."

"We found milk, eggs, basic necessities in the fridge. The electricity is on . . ."

"I look after the place for her. I sometimes . . . It's convenient . . ."

"Because she bought it at the time you moved here, isn't that right?"

"Yes, I helped negotiate the purchase."

"Did it seem like an odd purchase to you at the time?"

She didn't answer straightaway but unraveled the handkerchief and screwed it up into a ball again. "Why would you say that?"

"Well, it's the house where Sue was killed."

"I wouldn't know anything about that."

"Who chose the house, Sandy, her or you?"

"I'm . . ." She shook her head several times. "I'm not sure. It was a long time ago. Maybe I did."

"That's a hell of a coincidence, isn't it?"

"Not really. I mean, her brother had lived in this neighborhood. He mentioned it to her. When I came, I naturally . . ."

"You naturally chose a house across the street from Giorgio."

"I really don't know what you're driving at. I have just had the most appalling shock. I really need to rest."

"Of course. We'll leave you in peace. There is just one other question I would like to ask you before we go."

She sighed loudly and seemed to slump. "What is it, Detective?"

"Are you related to Mary, or are you just friends?"

She swallowed hard and looked down at the floor. "These questions. I have tried hard to be civil and polite. I know you're just doing your job, but I have to say I am finding these questions *very* intrusive."

"She was kind enough to give me a piece of thread that she had just sucked in order to put it through a needle. There was enough saliva there to get a DNA profile."

She stared hard at the floor, shook her head a couple of times. "No, no, this is wrong."

"We know that whoever killed Sue was closely related to Mary."

Again she shook her head but refused to look at me. "No."

"Did you kill Fernando, Sandy?"

"I don't like these questions. Please leave me alone."

"I called a friend at the bureau, asked him to check if you had a firearms license. I know you're a very good shot. I don't think many people realize just how good. But the way you shoot? That comes down to being really cold-blooded as much as anything else, doesn't it? What throws most people's aim in a critical moment is the emotions, their fear. But you don't have that problem. You don't feel that kind of emotion anymore, do you?"

"I don't want to answer these questions. Please go away."

"If I go away, I will have to take you with me." I waited a moment. She didn't say anything. I went on, "I understand that this was all about revenge. What I am not really clear about is whom you were avenging." Her eyes shifted to meet mine. "I mean," I said, "killing Fernando and Giorgio suggests that you were avenging Sue, but then, why did you kill Sue? If you killed her, what was to avenge?"

Again she didn't answer. The room was quiet for a moment, with only the crackle of the fire.

"But then I realized, you weren't avenging Sue at all, were you? You were punishing her." I paused a moment and said, "What happened to your ear?"

Her left hand went automatically to the large, blue enamel flower she had over her left earlobe. We looked at each other for a long moment. Then I said, "Yes, that ear." Still she didn't speak. "Fernando pulled out your earring, didn't he, when you stabbed him?"

She gave a couple of short nods.

"Why did you gut him?"

She spoke quietly, almost a whisper. "He deserved to be gutted, like a fish. He was so full of his own masculinity, always talking about how women loved his body. So full of his own sex, though he was actually bisexual. I wanted to cut it out of him and destroy it forever."

"The same as Giorgio."

"But Giorgio was worse. His big cock all over the place, making women love him, lying to them, lying with them, stealing their womanhood, lying on them, lying under them, lying inside them. He was the king of thieves. The king of liars."

"I thought you loved him."

"Not me."

"And Sue?"

She looked at my hands. Then her eyes traveled slowly up to my face and I knew she was thinking about killing me too. "She stole him."

"Everybody's stealing."

"Everybody is stealing from me."

"Do you know who you are?"

"That's a kind of crazy question."

"DNA, you know, can be virtually identical with identical twins."

"I know that."

"But fingerprints . . ."

Her gaze drifted. "Oh . . ."

"Fingerprints are different, even with identical twins." I waited a moment. "So do you know who you are?"

"I'm . . ." She took a very deep breath. "I feel very sleepy."

"I gave you a pen, remember?"

"Yes."

"And a card. You handled them both."

"Yes."

"I sent them to have the prints compared with the prints on Sue's throat. Sue was raped by a man. A man who left his semen inside her, and strangled her. So, again, do you remember who you are?"

Again the deep breath, the drifting gaze, a slight smile. "I don't always seem to be the same person."

"Do you remember the trip to Geneva?"

"I saved up for that for a long time. I had money saved too, from when Mommy died."

"You went to a clinic."

"It was there or the U.K. I preferred Geneva. It seemed . . . *cleaner.*"

"You understand that changing your sex does not change your identity."

She nodded. Then she shrugged. "But sometimes, changing your identity can change your sex."

I turned to Dehan, who was sitting very quietly. "Get a couple of the guys, will you?" She nodded and stood. I stood too and looked down at Sandy. "Cyril Browne, Sandy Beach, I am arresting you on five counts of murder. You do not have to say anything, but anything you do say may and will be taken down in evidence and used against you in a court of law."

EPILOGUE

THE SNOW WAS COMING DOWN HEAVIER. THROUGH THE window I could see the sidewalks blanketed in pristine white. There was not a soul on the streets, and the cars looked like icing sugar castellations fringing the roads. The fire was burning in the grate, and the room was warm and fragrant of roasting chicken. I turned as the back door opened and Dehan came in, stamping and puffing, with her shapeless wool hat on her head and a big, brown box in her arms.

"I always think," she said, "that a Christmas tree should look like a badly wrapped Christmas present. Over the top."

She grinned at me as she kicked the door closed, approached, and dumped the box on the sofa. "Mine's a martini, plenty dry. And put some tunes on, will'ya? I like that playlist with Bing and 'Santa Baby.' It reminds me of my dad. He loved all that . . ."

All this was said breathlessly as she opened the big carton and started pulling out armfuls of tinsel, intended for the big tree that stood by the window.

I went to my laptop, on the breakfast bar, and started searching while she pulled off her hat and coat and started hanging the first baubles. We were quiet for a moment. Then she stepped back, gazing at the big red ball she'd just hung, and sighed.

"I've been over it in my mind several times, Stone. I still don't get how you knew, so early on, that Sandy was Cyril."

The laptop started singing, "Booboom, booboom, booboom, booboom . . ." I went over to the sideboard and started mixing a martini, dry.

"I didn't know until later, but I suspected. The first thing that alerted me was the fact that the killer had made no effort at all to hide his identity, his fingerprints, and his DNA. If he had been caught immediately among the guests, or on CODIS or IAFIS, you just put it down to being stupid." I handed her her drink. "But he wasn't anywhere to be found. So that meant he wasn't stupid. And if somebody who isn't stupid is so brazen about their identity as to leave their prints and their DNA at a rape and murder scene, that can only mean they are extremely confident that they will never be found."

She sipped and shrugged. "Put like that . . ."

"It was also pretty obvious to me from the start that it had to be Cyril. In your words, Dehan, *entia non sunt multipilicanda praeter necesitatem.*"

"Yeah, go on, throw it in my face!"

I smiled and poured myself a Bushmills. "So the question I was wrestling with pretty much from the beginning was, what had Cyril done to be so confident his DNA and fingerprints would not trap him? Merry run-up to Christmas."

We toasted and sipped. I went and sat, enjoying the sight of her dressing the tree.

"Logically, it had to be something so radical that it was tantamount to a total change of identity. A change that would make any detective discard the possibility that he had raped and murdered her, out of hand. Becoming a woman would obviously do that. I confess, the idea was so extreme that for a while I couldn't accept it myself. That was why I was so keen to meet his sister and find out about his childhood."

The tree was taking shape as she draped a long string of gold tinsel from the top down in a wide spiral.

"What we found in Elk Grove seemed to confirm my theory, such as it was at that stage. He and his mother had been very close, like any mother and son. But he had then witnessed his mother die, if not at the hands of his father, certainly as a result of his father's rage. The experience had been deeply traumatic, and, as you saw yourself, his sister's tender mercies were not exactly therapeutic."

Dehan turned and nodded. "No, she seemed bent on destroying his identity, his self-esteem, and his independence."

"We'll never know for sure, but I suspect her father was a bit like that. The best way to control people is to destroy their belief in themselves. Poor Cyril had his belief in himself so deeply damaged that he turned to his dead mother to try and heal him. Consciously or unconsciously—probably both—he tried to follow her. In his words, he was trying to 'come home.'"

"Come home to his mother."

I nodded. "It's an expression that is full of symbolic meaning. He wants to return to his mother, he wants to return to a place that is safe, where he is loved and respected. The years following his mother's death, until he was finally able to leave home, must have been hell: a constant, systematic destruction of his self-esteem, being told day in and day out that he was an incompetent fantasist. And the more he sought solace in the memory of his mother, the more he was punished by his sister."

She sat on the arm of the chair facing me, with a strand of burgundy tinsel in her hands. "It's hard to imagine what that must be like."

"And I get the feeling that he was actually, potentially, an intelligent, motivated, able person. A fact which only added to the rage he was suppressing inside. By the time he got to New York, he was so badly damaged he didn't know who he was or how to get out of the crippling, paralyzing state he was in. He needed a therapist or a friend, somebody to guide him. But his personality was so awful that he couldn't make friends."

Dehan shook her head. "Along came Fernando."

"Yup, and he and Giorgio thought it was great sport to see him writhing in emotional agony as they dangled Sue in front of him. They could not have known that Sue was so similar to his mother. At first he adored her. But the more she flirted, however harmlessly, with Fernando and Giorgio, the more he relived the nightmare of his mother's betrayal and her death.

"I had a talk with his psychiatrist the other day, and he confirmed what I had suspected. In the end, Cyril's need for his mother, his obsession with her, became so all-consuming that he actually *became* her, both psychically and, as far as he could, physically. But he never quite stopped being himself either. On the one hand he had his own rage against his mother, like his father's rage, for betraying him, for abandoning him, for leaving him at the mercy of his sister.

"But on the other hand there was the rage against Jose Rodriguez too, the journalist his mother had her affair with. Jose Rodriguez was the ultimate symbol of his own inadequacy and weakness. Jose Rodriguez was this big, neon sign that said, 'Cyril Browne is not a man.'

"It's not hard to see how he projected that onto Fernando and Giorgio. Sue, Fernando, and Giorgio represented his darkest daemons, and he raged against all three of them."

She had hung a large, acid-yellow ball and now stood staring at her warped reflection in it. "Okay," she said, "I get that. But first of all, why, after killing Sue, did he A, come back and B, wait twelve years to kill Giorgio and Fernando?"

"That is something his psychiatrist is trying to find out now, but my guess is this. As you suspected, Sue started befriending him, not realizing that this act of kindness would actually trigger his rage against her. Because one minute she was being sweet and nice to him, and the next moment she would be flirting with Giorgio and Fernando. They would be coming on to her in an overtly sexual way, and she would laugh. This is like his deepest, darkest nightmares coming to life in front of him. It's his mother's betrayal all over again. This is where his neurosis starts to turn into a full-blown psychosis and his mother starts to come to life inside his own psyche. He loves her and needs her so badly, the only way to escape her betrayal is to become her. And this is where he decides that what he wants is to have a sex change operation, and he books a clinic in Geneva.

"I don't know if he planned to kill her that Halloween. We'll probably never know for sure, but Dr. Petersen speculates that the unconscious motivation was probably there, and that was what drove him to be at the party that night. It wasn't part of a conscious plan, but it was an unconscious motivation that would strike given the opportunity."

"Hence the apparent discrepancy between handing in notice and the opportunistic nature of the murder."

"Exactly. So when she left, and he saw that Fernando had not stayed with her, he called on her, ostensibly to see if she was okay. She let him in. They were in the bedroom. Did she invite him in? Did he come on to her? The thing is, at some point that sexual charge was ignited, and he killed her. Ironically, exactly contrary to your theory, the only cure for his erectile dysfunction was to release his repressed rage."

Dehan rolled her eyes. "Go Carmen. So he went home. His bags were probably already packed, and he went back to his sister's place in a state of turmoil. He had satisfied his drive to kill Sue, but was now tortured by remorse."

"Something like that, but his psychosis was driving him by now. Remorse was something that was fading in him. His psychosis drove him to fake his own death in Reno, and then fly to Geneva for his surgery. It was the fact that he left his jacket so conveniently to be found on the rubble, and so helpfully registered as having no next of kin, that made me suspect that he had not really committed suicide at all. I was convinced Joe White didn't see him jump. He assumed he jumped, and then imagined that's what he'd seen. At that distance, running in the dark, in a panic, trying not to trip and talking on the phone, he had no idea what he'd seen. Cyril threw something heavy into the cement and jumped over the fence. That simple. He was very cold-blooded.

"I suspect that, at that stage, his fantasy was to return as Sandy Beach, and kill Giorgio and Fernando in the same place where he had killed Sue, back in her apartment in the Bronx. His hatred for Giorgio must have been very intense at that time, and these symbolic elements must have been very important to him. These were the psychotic, ritualistic elements to his killing which I mentioned in the beginning, which suggested a serial killer. But, curiously, by the time he'd had his operations and completed his transformation, it seems that his drive to kill Giorgio and Fernando started gradually to subside. It was as though it belonged to his previous self, to Cyril. By becoming his mother, he had found some kind of meaning and peace.

"So when he eventually returned to the Bronx, I think he did actually start to fall in love with Giorgio. Perhaps he was living out his mother's need to have an affair with some kind of artistic, creative bad boy, like her journalist. Whatever the reason, his fantasy about killing them seems to have faded for a few years."

"So why *did* he kill them?"

I nodded. "I have a theory about that. She had been hanging around Giorgio for about eight or nine years, but she didn't know Fernando that well. I suspect that as she got closer to Giorgio, and they started having their little affair, she began to realize that he and Fernando were more than just friends. That must have stirred long buried feelings—feelings that belonged to Cyril—and when we came along and started digging things up, and she discovered that they were both dangerous, and involved with prostitutes, Cyril's original hatred and murderous intent were fully reawakened. She desperately wanted Giorgio to be a man she could fall in love with, but he wasn't. He was exactly the kind of man Cyril hated for taking his mother away from him. So he and Fernando both had to die."

She sipped her drink, gazing at the fire. "You were so convinced," she said after a while, "that Sandy was Cyril. I can see all your reasoning, but even if I had followed it at the time, I would not have been *that* convinced, that sure, that she was Cyril."

I shrugged. "I suspected it, but you're right. In the end I was certain. And there was a reason for that."

"What?"

I smiled. "Well, we had two murders committed by the same person, but one was committed by a man and the other was committed by a woman. There was only one way that could happen: Cyril had had a sex change operation and come back. The only person that could possibly be Cyril was Sandy."

"You make it sound almost logical."

"It's not logical for us. But to his psychotic mind, at the time, it was logical. One of the problems was that in the intervening years, his psychosis had receded. So we were looking at the actions of a psychotic person, who was, in many ways, no longer psychotic."

"So if we had left the case alone...?"

I shook my head. "I don't think so. There are signs that her split personality was still active. I think she kept Sue's house as a place where she could still be Cyril. I think she used to go there to vent Cyril's fantasies, as a kind of escape vale. The homicidal rage was still there, it was just waiting to be ignited."

"Wow..."

There was a ping from the kitchen. She looked up and smiled. "The chicken is done. Let's eat, Mr. Stone."

I drained my glass and stood, and looked at the table we had set, with a red Christmas candle, holly, and the tree reflecting off the wineglasses.

Me and Dehan. This was home.

Don't miss BLOOD INTO WINE. The riveting sequel in the Dead Cold Mystery series.

Scan the QR code below to purchase BLOOD INTO WINE.

Or go to: righthouse.com/blood-into-wine

NOTE: flip to the very end to read an exclusive sneak peak...

DON'T MISS ANYTHING!

If you want to stay up to date on all new releases in this series, with this author, or with any of our new deals, you can do so by joining our newsletters below.

In addition, you will immediately gain access to our entire *Right House VIP Library,* which includes many riveting Mystery and Thriller novels for your enjoyment!

righthouse.com/email

(Easy to unsubscribe. No spam. Ever.)

ALSO BY BLAKE BANNER

Up to date books can be found at:
www.righthouse.com/blake-banner

ROGUE THRILLERS
Gates of Hell (Book 1)
Hell's Fury (Book 2)

ALEX MASON THRILLERS
Odin (Book 1)
Ice Cold Spy (Book 2)
Mason's Law (Book 3)
Assets and Liabilities (Book 4)
Russian Roulette (Book 5)
Executive Order (Book 6)
Dead Man Talking (Book 7)
All The King's Men (Book 8)
Flashpoint (Book 9)
Brotherhood of the Goat (Book 10)
Dead Hot (Book 11)
Blood on Megiddo (Book 12)
Son of Hell (Book 13)

HARRY BAUER THRILLER SERIES
Dead of Night (Book 1)
Dying Breath (Book 2)
The Einstaat Brief (Book 3)
Quantum Kill (Book 4)
Immortal Hate (Book 5)
The Silent Blade (Book 6)
LA: Wild Justice (Book 7)

Breath of Hell (Book 8)
Invisible Evil (Book 9)
The Shadow of Ukupacha (Book 10)
Sweet Razor Cut (Book 11)
Blood of the Innocent (Book 12)
Blood on Balthazar (Book 13)
Simple Kill (Book 14)
Riding The Devil (Book 15)
The Unavenged (Book 16)
The Devil's Vengeance (Book 17)
Bloody Retribution (Book 18)
Rogue Kill (Book 19)
Blood for Blood (Book 20)

DEAD COLD MYSTERY SERIES
An Ace and a Pair (Book 1)
Two Bare Arms (Book 2)
Garden of the Damned (Book 3)
Let Us Prey (Book 4)
The Sins of the Father (Book 5)
Strange and Sinister Path (Book 6)
The Heart to Kill (Book 7)
Unnatural Murder (Book 8)
Fire from Heaven (Book 9)
To Kill Upon A Kiss (Book 10)
Murder Most Scottish (Book 11)
The Butcher of Whitechapel (Book 12)
Little Dead Riding Hood (Book 13)
Trick or Treat (Book 14)
Blood Into Wine (Book 15)
Jack In The Box (Book 16)
The Fall Moon (Book 17)
Blood In Babylon (Book 18)
Death In Dexter (Book 19)
Mustang Sally (Book 20)

A Christmas Killing (Book 21)
Mommy's Little Killer (Book 22)
Bleed Out (Book 23)
Dead and Buried (Book 24)
In Hot Blood (Book 25)
Fallen Angels (Book 26)
Knife Edge (Book 27)
Along Came A Spider (Book 28)
Cold Blood (Book 29)
Curtain Call (Book 30)

THE OMEGA SERIES
Dawn of the Hunter (Book 1)
Double Edged Blade (Book 2)
The Storm (Book 3)
The Hand of War (Book 4)
A Harvest of Blood (Book 5)
To Rule in Hell (Book 6)
Kill: One (Book 7)
Powder Burn (Book 8)
Kill: Two (Book 9)
Unleashed (Book 10)
The Omicron Kill (Book 11)
9mm Justice (Book 12)
Kill: Four (Book 13)
Death In Freedom (Book 14)
Endgame (Book 15)

ABOUT US

Right House is an independent publisher created by authors for readers. We specialize in Action, Thriller, Mystery, and Crime novels.

If you enjoyed this novel, then there is a good chance you will like what else we have to offer! Please stay up to date by using any of the links below.

Join our mailing lists to stay up to date -->
righthouse.com/email
Visit our website --> righthouse.com
Contact us --> contact@righthouse.com

 facebook.com/righthousebooks
X x.com/righthousebooks
instagram.com/righthousebooks

EXCLUSIVE SNEAK PEAK OF...

BLOOD INTO WINE

CHAPTER 1

Deputy Inspector John Newman entered the detectives' room on hesitant feet, looking this way and that with small, jerky movements of his head, like a chicken on a secret mission. He bore a slim manila file. He saw me watching from my desk, smiled with relief, and approached.

"John," he said, "I thought I'd find you here."

I wagged my pencil at him. "That's because it's the detectives' room, and I am a detective."

He smiled as though he knew it was a joke but wasn't sure why it was funny. Dehan glanced at me from under her eyebrows then smiled at the inspector.

"Good morning, sir."

"Carmen!" He looked at her in what you could only describe as alarm. "Naturally I was looking for you both! I just happened to see . . ." He swallowed and changed tack. "I like to get out of my office from time to time, see the troops, haha . . ."

I smiled amiably. "Here we are, sir, trooping."

"Indeed! And what are you working on?"

I gestured at the old cartons on the desk. "We were just looking through the cold cases, sir. We were thinking about the

Vince Wolowitz case. They found him tied to his bed in his house on St. Lawrence Avenue."

Dehan nodded. "Clason Point, near the Catholic church. His dog had eaten his foot."

The inspector winced. I contributed, "The neighbors said he had a hundred grand in a box under his bed, but it was never found."

Dehan sat back. "August ninety-seven. I always had a theory about his family."

I wagged my pencil at her. "I've been meaning to look into that angle for some time."

The inspector's smile had turned to a rictus, which is not a good thing to happen to a smile.

"If you haven't started on it yet, I wonder if you would have a look at the Jose Robles case?" he said.

Dehan frowned. "That's cold? What'd they do, keep it in the fridge overnight?"

"I think what Detective Dehan means, sir . . ."

"I know what she means, John, and she is quite right." He pulled a chair over from Mo's desk and sat heavily. "The case is not even a week old. But it has run into some . . ." He hesitated, then plunged on. ". . . well, *problems,* which seem intractable. And frankly, I am under pressure from 'above'"—he made little inverted commas with his fingers—"to get it solved 'pronto.'" He did it again, hunching his shoulders a little. "You two," he said, gazing out the window, "seem to have a way of unearthing clues that don't appear even to be there."

"Why thank you, sir." I smiled. "I think so too."

"So, I know it's not strictly a cold case, but I'd be grateful if you'd have a look at it."

He tossed the file in front of me on the desk, and I leaned over and picked it up. "Who had it to start with?"

"Gutierrez, but he's glad to let it go because, as far as *he's* concerned, it's closed. And I have to say . . ."

He hesitated again. Dehan frowned at him. She said, "You

agree . . ." He shrugged. She pressed him. "So why are we looking at it? What is the intractable problem?"

He sighed. "ADA Costas Varoufakis."

Her eyebrows seemed to levitate. "Assistant District Attorney Costas Varu . . . The assistant district attorney is the intractable problem?"

"He does not believe it should be closed."

Suddenly I was interested. I leaned forward. "On what grounds? And since when does the assistant district attorney decide when we close a case?"

"Since his uncle went to school with the mayor."

I grunted. "And his grounds?"

He made a face of helplessness and spread his hands. "It seems they were friends. They shared an interest in Mediterranean history or something."

I made a dubious expression with my eyebrows and offered it to Dehan. She copied it and offered it back. The inspector sighed. "Look, I'm sorry, and I am aware it's an imposition. Just work your magic on it for a day or two, and if you are convinced it's case closed, we close the case and you can get on with . . ."

He made little stirring motions with his finger. I said, "Vince Wolowitz."

"Indeed."

"Of course we will. I shall enter it into my little black book of favors to be called in at a later time, sir."

"He's joking, sir," said Dehan, in a way that said that I wasn't.

He nodded and smiled, and retreated up to the rarified atmosphere of the upper floor. I took the photos from the file and tossed the rest at Dehan. She read as I looked.

"Jose Robles, a Spanish national."

I spoke, looking at a photograph of him. "Spanish from Spain?"

She stared at me a moment. "Yes, Spanish from Spain. PhD in applied physics from the University of Santiago de Compostela, Galicia. That's also in Spanish Spain."

"I know. I've been. Excellent seafood."

"He was conducting research and lecturing at University College New York, in Manhattan. He'd been here a year last September and had another year to run."

The photograph I was looking at was a head and shoulders portrait. I figured he was thirty-something, and he was handsome in that Mediterranean kind of way that women find so appealing: dark, chiseled features, black hair, and big, brown eyes that managed to be both sweet and insolent at the same time. His hair was receding slightly, and the collar of his pink shirt was on the outside of his turquoise cashmere sweater. He wasn't smiling.

Dehan was saying, "He was found December fourth, that's last Tuesday, at the house of a friend, Agnes Shine, also a lecturer at the university. He had been shot eight times in the thorax with a 9mm Sig Sauer Tacops P226..."

We both looked up, stared at each other, and frowned. She raised her eyebrows and went back to reading. I stared at the naked trees outside, then turned back to the photos and found the one of Dr. Jose Robles lying sprawled and dead in an armchair. I was looking at the blood on his chest.

"The weapon was recovered at the scene..."

"Dropped on the floor near the body."

"Correct. It was sent for prints and still awaiting results."

"What about Agnes Shine?"

"I'm coming to that, big guy. She was known to be a close friend of the victim. Dr. Patricia Meigh, Jose's head of department..."

"Me?"

"Meigh, M-E-I-G-H, Meigh, she's the head of the department that was conducting the research that Jose was involved in. She was concerned when Jose didn't turn up Monday morning and wouldn't answer his phone. She tried to locate Agnes Shine, but it turned out she hadn't shown up either..."

"What's her department?"

"Um . . ." She scanned several pages. "Professor of Economics and International Finance."

"Huh, okay."

"She didn't turn up either. Tuesday they were both missing again, so Dr. Meigh raised the alarm. A patrol car was dispatched to his house with no result. Her house is a few doors down, so they went to have a look. Living room is on the second floor, but there are outside stairs. They saw him through the window."

"The drapes were open."

"Presumably."

"They were." I waved the photograph at her.

"Uh-huh. Stephens Avenue, right by Pugsley Creek Park. Officers forced their way in, found the victim deceased at eleven a.m., and no trace of Agnes. No driver's license or any other kind of ID was found at the house. Her purse was also missing, leading Detective Gutierrez to conclude that she had killed Jose in a fit of passion and fled."

"Witnesses?"

"Uniforms canvassed the neighbors, but nobody saw or heard anything out of the ordinary. Jose was last seen by a friend at the university Friday evening at eight. So time of death is sometime between Friday at eight p.m. and Tuesday at eleven in the morning."

She dropped the file and reached across to pick up the photographs. I sat drumming my fingers on the desk and gazing at the stark, gray sky outside. "It has, as Holmes would say, some interesting features. Was the Sig registered to either of them?"

She answered while staring at the photograph of Jose Robles, dead in the chair. "Nope. Unregistered."

"Curiouser and curiouser."

"You're mixing your quotes. That's *Alice in Wonderland*."

I stood and grabbed my coat. "Come, Dehan, I want to have a look at the crime scene. For once it is less than ten years old. It might actually tell us something."

"I'm giddy with excitement," she said with no particular

expression and gathered up the papers and photographs into the file.

She pulled on a thick coat, a brown-and-white angora wool hat, and matching gloves, and we went to collect the keys to the properties. Then we made our way out into the ice-cold street. There was no snow, but what moisture there was on the roads had frozen and had the brittle look of thin ice. We crossed to my ancient Jaguar—an authentic, right-hand-drive, burgundy Mark II from 1964, with leather seats and walnut trim—and climbed in. As we slammed the doors, shutting out the icy air, Dehan said, "I can see why Varou . . . the ADA."

"Varoufakis."

I fired up the engine and reversed out of the lot. Dehan was still talking.

"I can see why he's not satisfied. A Sig Sauer Tacops P226, new, is going to cost you over a grand. It's a serious pro's weapon, favored by special ops units like the SEALS and Delta Force. You can pick up a Glock 17, which is a damn good gun, for half the price. Or a Taurus, which is okay, for half that again. So what is Dr. Agnes Shine doing with a thousand-buck weapon that isn't registered to her, or anybody else?"

I turned from Story onto Soundview and made a "hmmm . . ." noise. "Did you look at the photograph of him?"

"Which one?"

"The portrait." She watched me but didn't say anything. "He looks to me like the kind of man who might own an expensive gun. Possibly he wouldn't own a gun, but if he did, he would buy an expensive one."

"You can tell that from his portrait photograph?"

"Sure. You don't believe me? What is the betting he drove a German car?"

"*What . . . ?*"

"Come on, what do *you* think he drove?"

"I have no idea, Stone."

"Audis are too common for him, likewise Mercedes, and VW. Porsche is out of his price range. BMW. The three-twenty, in . . ."

"Come on!"

"Wait—in white."

"That's ridiculous."

"Not at all. He wears a pink shirt with a turquoise cashmere sweater, and he has the collar on the outside. That kind of thing can tell you a lot about a man and his relationship with his mother: he is vain, showy, has poor judgment, bad taste, and he believes he is entitled to the best because Mommy told him so."

She sighed and shook her head. "Anyway, okay, so maybe the gun was his. Still, it is odd that it was not registered."

"Laws are pretty tight here. Still, I take your point, if he had one, you'd expect it to be legal. By the way, what did you think about the picture of him in the chair, shot?"

She leafed through them till she'd found it. She was quiet for a moment, examining it.

"Not a lot. They'd been drinking. He has a glass of wine beside him." She leafed through them again and looked at another picture. "There is another glass on the table beside the sofa. They were both sent for fingerprinting, and the bottle."

"What's the wine?"

"The wine?"

"Yes, what is it? California, Chile, French . . . ?"

She peered at the picture. "It looks like . . . Bogle Vineyards, 2016. Is that important?"

"California. It might be, Little Grasshopper."

"Whatever . . . It was sent for fingerprinting too. What else? Nothing much. Why? Am I missing some cigarette ash or something? Are you going to identify the killer by the texture of the burned paper?"

"That vitriol which is drooling from your lips, Detective Dehan, will come back to burn you in the ass. We are here."

I pulled into Patterson Avenue and, as we crossed into

Compton and Stephens, we were suddenly in a country village somewhere in New England. I smiled. "I love these little corners of the Bronx, don't you, Dehan? You're in this vast city, with millions of people around you, and yet you could be in rural Maine."

She cocked an eyebrow at me. "Is this what they call being whimsical, Stone? Are you feeling whimsical today? You haven't got a craving for tinned peaches and oysters, have you? Tell me you're not pregnant."

I chortled good-humoredly and slowed outside a large clapboard house on three floors plus an attic, with yellow tape across the porch. The house was part of a row of four that were all oddly grotesque but somehow managed to be attractive. Everywhere about them was a superabundance of foliage from the woodland in the park at the back of the houses.

"That's his house, right?"

"Uh-uh. Hers is the first on the left, after the trees, about two hundred yards down."

Agnes' house was, like all the houses on Stephens Avenue, peculiar. It was set behind a chain-link fence and gate, beyond a large lawn that must have been thirty yards long at the very least, and a good fifteen yards across. Like Jose's house, it was clapboard but seemed to be put together from bits that were left over from other clapboard houses.

It had a gable roof and also a flat roof, an arch over a carport, a chimney that ran all the way up the outside of the house, right beside the front door, and a flight of six substantial stone steps up to that door. I was still trying to work out how the fireplace could be next to the front door when I noticed a broad flight of wooden steps going up to the second story, on the outside of the carport. It was like something from the Picasso school of abstract architecture.

Here too there was yellow tape across the chain-link fence, and also across the front porch. We climbed out, and the slam of the car doors echoed across the icy morning. A couple of ravens, scared by the reports, flapped darkly away toward Pugsley Creek

Park. The lawn was well tended, the frosty grass was short and was obviously mowed regularly, but there were no flower beds, no trees, no bench for sitting out in the evening.

We crossed the front yard. Dehan pulled away the tape from the door, unlocked it, and we stepped inside. It was dark, and there was a silence in the place that comes with death. It was a quiet saturated with stillness. The door that had mystified me turned out to be the kitchen door. The kitchen, along with the dining area, took up the whole of the ground floor, and the chimney I'd seen from the car was a flue that rose from an old, blue iron range that stood to the right as you went in. It looked like an antique, and it was spotless.

The floors were hardwood and highly polished. There was a table in the middle of the floor with four chairs placed evenly around it. A doily in the exact center held a vase of plastic flowers. There was an oak dresser against one wall that also appeared to be an antique. Beside it, a wine rack held twenty-four bottles of wine. I examined them. They were all Spanish, twelve from Rioja and twelve from Ribera del Duero.

After that, I went methodically through the drawers. They were well ordered and, like everything else in the kitchen, very clean. Dehan was watching me with her hands in her back pockets.

"What are you looking for?"

"Agnes Shine."

"You think she's hiding in the cutlery drawer?"

"This house belongs to a highly ordered eccentric who doesn't like high-maintenance relationships."

She smiled and pulled off her hat. "You're something, Stone."

"No flowers." I pointed at the vase. "Plastic."

An arch in the left-hand wall gave onto a narrow entrance with a door into the carport and a flight of stairs that led to the upper floor. These were wood too, and carpeted in an ugly dark green. They creaked as we climbed.

On the upper floor, there was a landing. At the back, there

were two bedrooms and a bathroom. The front of the house was taken up by a large living room. Here there was an open fireplace with a white marble surround. Another antique. Two tall windows overlooked the long lawn and the street. There were low, heavy wooden bookcases along all the walls, holding books on just about everything, but there was no fiction. Nor were there ornaments, nor pictures on the walls. There were four large, attractive lamps, evenly spaced, and a single overhead bulb with a green shade.

An old television was positioned in the corner, near the fireplace. Opposite, there was a brown sofa upholstered in suede. On either side, at an angle, there were two matching armchairs. One of them was caked with dry blood and peppered with small, black holes.

The silence was total.

Dehan pointed at the windows. "Triple glazing. Probably why the neighbors didn't hear anything."

I nodded and took my pen from my inside pocket. I crouched down beside the chair and slipped my pen into three of the bullet holes. Dehan said, "What?"

I shook my head and made a "nothing" face, then stood. "The sofa and the chairs, they are based on the design of Coco Chanel's sofa at the Ritz. They are very good imitations. That's buffalo hide. You're looking at sixty thousand bucks' worth of furniture right there, Dehan."

"Sixty grand?"

I nodded. "So he's sitting in that chair. He's got a glass of wine on that table, beside him. According to the photograph, she's probably sitting on that chair on the other side of the sofa, because that's where the other glass was, and the bottle. Does that seem odd to you?"

"A little." She shrugged. "But she's mad at him, remember? Usually they'd probably both be snuggled up on the sofa, watching a movie or something. But today she's mad at him. So they're a bit uptight, formal, they're sitting on chairs having what he thinks is going to be an adult conversation to sort out their problems. Instead, she's got this Sig."

I nodded. "She's got it here, concealed somewhere, ready to shoot him, or maybe she's left it in her room. She's thinking if he comes through, she'll forgive him. But he doesn't, he just makes her mad, so she gets up, goes to her room, collects the weapon, comes back, and lets rip."

"Eight shots, that's a pretty mad woman."

"Yeah. From the photograph, I'd say she was standing here, in the middle of the floor."

I positioned myself halfway between the two chairs, about seven or eight feet from where Jose had been sitting. Dehan frowned. "So that looks like she went and got the gun, right? Because if she was sitting in the other chair, where her glass was, why would she get up and go over there to shoot him? And, if she had, he would have got up, tried to run or take the gun. So like you said, she's left the room, got the weapon, and come back to where you are, and shot him."

I nodded slowly, looked around the room, and stared at Dehan. "There are several things troubling me, Dehan, but you know what's troubling me the most?"

She smiled. "No, but two gets you twenty it'll be something that annoys me."

"I can't even *smell* a motive."

CHAPTER 2

She pulled off her coat, walked away, and stood staring out at the street. Her silhouette against the cold, gray light was long and slim. After a moment, she turned and sat on the windowsill.

"They were close. They were probably having an affair. He was going to ditch her, or there was another woman—story as old as hormones. We don't know anything about them yet."

"I know . . ." I looked around the room. "But does this look to you like a place where there was a crime of passion? Even the wineglasses have coasters."

"What are you getting at?"

"I don't know. The wineglasses have coasters, everything is neat and tidy, and yet she has blown eight holes in her twenty-thousand-dollar suede chair. And she has used a silencer."

"How the hell do you know that? There's triple glazing . . ."

"A fact which she would have known. But the penetration, from a 9mm Sig, there would have been deeper penetration into the chair, I think. The silencer reduces the velocity of the bullet."

I crossed the landing to the bedroom. The drapes were closed. They too were a dark green, and thin cracks of green light glowed down their sides from the park woodland outside. The bed was made and uncreased. I went into the en suite bathroom. There was a shower cubicle, but no bath. The towels were all folded and clean. There was a shower gel scented with lime and lavender, and an anti-frizz shampoo for extra body. And there were a lot of other things I had started to find in my own bathroom since I had married Dehan.

I stepped out of the bathroom and saw Dehan with her arms crossed, leaning against the doorjamb, looking down at the bed.

"I know what you mean," she said. "There is no disorder."

"The only disorder is the killing." I thought a moment. "The killing, and the fact that she is missing. We may find she's a little OCD when we talk to her workmates."

"Mm-hm. I think you're right."

"This place has nothing to tell me, Dehan. Which, in itself, says something, but I'm not sure what yet. Let's take a walk and see what his house has to say."

We stepped out into the cold, still air and walked, hunched into our coats, the two hundred yards back up the road to Jose Robles' house. This house was, again, peculiar. The first floor was made of raw stone, like big rocks cemented together then filed down so they were flat. It was indescribably ugly. A flight of steps, which looked like something out of a medieval castle, rose to the front door, not directly, but across the facade of the house; and that front door was not at ground level, but on the second floor. The third floor and the attic were all clapboard, like the back of the house.

As we approached, breathing great clouds of condensation, Dehan, whose nose and cheeks had turned red under her hat, said, "Do you think these houses were designed in the sixties, and the architects were all high on acid?"

"It would explain a lot."

We turned in off the sidewalk and headed for the stairs. Just to the left of them was a double garage. I stopped, took hold of Dehan's elbow, and pointed. She stared, then looked me in the face and emitted a high-pitched laugh, which she kept going all the way up the steps to the front door. The reason for her laughter was the white BMW 320 which was parked outside the garage.

She opened the door and we went in. The front door gave directly onto the living room. It was a style that in the late '60s and early '70s would have been considered modern. The walls were paneled in tongue and groove, the fireplace was stone, and the furniture was all low and leather, though none of it was of the class or quality of Agnes' stuff.

There were many lamps, of all kinds of shapes and sizes, mostly pretentious and all of it expensive. There was a large coffee table in the middle of the floor that seemed to be made out of hunks of driftwood, and there were books, lots of them, stuffed into every available nook and cranny. Most of them were in Spanish, but a good number of professional reference books were in English. Open on the table was the *Journal of the Electrochemical Society*. I picked it up and had a look at what he was reading: "The Development and Future of Lithium Ion Batteries," by George E. Blomgren. It didn't mean much to me. I put it back down and continued looking around. He had a well-stocked bar, and there was a lot of soot in the fire.

I pointed at the alcoves on either side of the fire, where cabinets and shelves had been put in. "Unlike her, he has photographs."

She moved over and started looking at them, muttering, "Yeah, Agnes didn't have any. That was odd."

I went and hunkered down by the fire. I took the poker from the stand and started poking around in the soot. There were still a few hunks of blackened wood that had not burned completely. I stood and looked at his collection of bottles. He had Tio Pepe dry sherry, Martini, Gordon's Gin, Beefeater, Glenfiddich Scotch whiskey, and Johnnie Walker Red Label.

Dehan spoke suddenly, still looking at the photographs. "Looks like his family. That looks like his mother and his father and a bunch of friends. They're cooking paella out in the country. That guy has to be his brother."

I stood and looked over her shoulder. "Why?"

"Looks like him, and he's in these pictures too. The Spanish are Mediterranean, they are very family oriented. Look, see that pretty girl there? She looks like me. That's his sister."

I ruffled her head and told her she was cute and made my way across the large room into the kitchen. There was no door separating the two rooms; it was just another space, sectioned off.

A heavy crystal tumbler stood beside the sink. I picked it up and smelled it. It smelled of whiskey. I opened the dishwasher. There was nothing inside it. He had a big, silver fridge and beside it a wine rack. Like Agnes', it held two dozen bottles in it, mainly red, all from Rioja or Ribera del Duero in Spain.

I leaned my ass against the work surface and crossed my arms. Dehan walked in. I scratched my Adam's apple.

"It was cold. He had a fire burning, yet her drapes were open. He was drinking whiskey and reading his journal. Somebody or something disturbed him. He set down his journal and brought his empty glass to the kitchen, then, presumably, made his way to Agnes' house. There they drank wine and she shot him, with a suppressed Sig, while the drapes were open."

"It is odd. I see where the ADA is coming from. We need Robles' phone records, and hers, see if she called him. If we can establish that she called him over the weekend, that will help narrow down time of death. I'll get on that." As an afterthought, she added, "The lab has his cell."

She walked away dialing and I made my way up to the next floor, to the bedrooms and the bathrooms. There was a landing that ran from front to back. At the far end, the passage made a dogleg and a further flight rose to the attic.

There were three bedrooms. Two were clearly guest rooms and had signs of having been used occasionally, perhaps by his Mediterranean family-oriented family. His room, the master bedroom, had red satin sheets on the bed, a Spanish translation of a Stephen King novel on the bedside table, and an electronic clock with an alarm set for six a.m. In a laundry basket he had some dirty linens, including more sheets. These were in black satin.

I checked his wardrobe and found a handful of good, off-the-peg suits, several pairs of Levi's, several cashmere sweaters in dubious colors, and lots of expensive shirts. His shoes were real leather and handmade. There was nothing else.

I explored both bathrooms. There was nothing of interest there either. I sat on the stairs and thought about that and decided that, like at Agnes' house, the absence of anything interesting was interesting in itself. Downstairs I could hear Dehan talking. When she had finished, I rose and made my way down. She met me at the foot of the stairs. There we stood, staring at each other as I sucked my teeth.

"If they were lovers, Dehan, and I am not saying they weren't, they had a very sterile, clinical relationship. There is no sign of his presence in her house, and no sign of her presence in his house. Where the hell did they have sex? Unless they had a third dwelling somewhere, where they used to meet up and get all their primal urges out of their system, these kids were not involved with each other. Not in any meaningful sense of the word."

She was staring at me with narrowed eyes. "I know," she said. "I was thinking the same thing. But if they weren't involved, why the hell did she kill him?"

I shrugged. "There is always the other Big Motive."

"Money?"

"What else? Or, it may not have been her. Gutierrez assumes it was her because she has vanished, but we haven't got the prints back yet. We don't know if her prints are on the gun or not."

"That's true. She may have vanished because she's dead."

I sighed and shook my head. "But that does present us with a different problem. When people kill for money, or power, it tends to be premeditated and more or less carefully planned. When people pump other people full of lead, drop the weapon, and run, that tends to be a killing motivated by rage, jealousy, vengeance—sex. Something that makes you temporarily lose control."

She slapped me on the shoulder. "Let's go talk to Frank, drop in on the lab while we're there." She opened the door and we stepped out into the icy morning again. "Did you look at the lock at Agnes' place?"

"Yup." I thrust my hands in my pockets as we made our way down the castle steps and started walking back toward the car. "It wasn't forced. And as Jose was not actually at his own house, that means either A, the killer was a third party and Agnes let him in, or B, it was Agnes."

"Him or her." She said it after a long silence as she walked around the car with her hands in her pockets, her shoulders hunched and her collar up, then sniffed. We climbed in and slammed the doors. I turned the key and the big old engine roared into life.

"We should also remember," I said, "that they are both academics. And academics are all more or less crazy."

She was nodding as I pulled away and headed toward White Plains Road. "This is a guy who sits down in front of the fire, with a glass of single malt, and reads about batteries."

We took it easy, and, twenty minutes later, we found Frank in his office, behind a steel desk, going through papers. He looked up as we came in, frowned, and said, "What?"

Dehan sat without being invited. She still had her hands in her pockets and her shoulders hunched. I stayed in his doorway and smiled at him.

"Good morning, Frank. Jose Robles, multiple gunshot wounds to the chest, Stephens Avenue . . ."

"I know who Jose Robles is, John. I thought Gutierrez had that case. Surely it hasn't gone cold already! I haven't even sent him my results yet!"

"It's the weather, Frank. It's making everything cold. We got handed the case. What can I tell you? Or, more to the point, what can you tell us?"

He shook his head at Dehan across the desk. "It's his wit that makes him so endearing."

He finished shuffling papers and stood, went to an "out" tray on top of a filing cabinet, took a manila envelope, and handed it to Dehan.

"We haven't got a sample of Agnes Shine's fingerprints, but from samples taken from her office and her house, we have isolated some prints that offer an extremely high probability of being hers. They are, however, suggestive and not admissible as evidence."

Dehan nodded and reluctantly extracted a hand from her pocket to take the envelope. "Obviously," she said.

"What can I tell you?" He sighed. "The gun, a Sig Sauer Tacops P226, an unusual choice for a crime of passion. Based on the prints, it was fired by the person we assume to be Agnes Shine. We can say with absolute certainty that the person who fired the gun was a frequent visitor to Agnes' office and her home, almost certainly her. She also handled the bottle and one of the glasses found at the scene."

He dropped back into his chair. "What else? There is very little else. He was shot eight times at close range. He could have died from any one of the wounds, which perforated his liver, his stomach, his lungs, and his heart..."

I leaned my shoulder on the doorjamb. "But the one that killed him was the one to the heart."

"Indeed."

"So I guess you haven't examined the contents of his stomach."

He managed to scowl and raise an eyebrow at the same time. "Can you think of a reason why I would have?"

I nodded. "Yeah, I'd like to know what he had for his last supper."

"You're serious."

"I am."

"Anything else you'd like me to waste the taxpayers' dollars on?"

"No . . . I'd be curious to know if he'd had sex before getting shot, but my other questions are for Joe."

He frowned. "Really? I don't know what you're looking for, John, but I have seen many crimes of passion in my time, and this murder is entirely consistent."

"Almost. Have a look in his belly for me, will you?"

"What do you mean, 'almost'?"

I smiled. "Well, there's the gun, and then there's the sequence of the shots."

Dehan turned in her chair to stare at me. The expression on her face was an echo of the one on Frank's. He said, "Sequence? What sequence?"

Dehan shrugged. "What sequence, Stone?"

"The shot to the heart, the one that killed him, was also the first shot."

"Excuse me?"

"None of the other wounds bled anywhere near as profusely. The first shot stopped his heart pumping. So the first shot, delivered with a suppressed Sig Sauer P226—the pro's choice—hit him in the heart and killed him."

Dehan blinked a lot. Frank sighed. "Is there anything else you'd like to tell me? The person who pulled the trigger on that gun has a ninety-nine-point-nine percent chance of being Dr. Agnes Shine. Now go away, please."

I smiled and looked at my watch. "We'd better leave before I upset him. We need to go and see Dr. Meigh, and on the way I need to call Joe."

Frank shrugged. "Joe'll tell you the same thing." To Dehan he said, "I only work with him. You married him."

On the way out, I tossed Dehan the keys. "Let's go see Dr. Meigh."

She climbed behind the wheel, and I got in the passenger seat and called Joe at the lab as she pulled out of the lot and onto Morris Park Avenue.

"Yeah?"

"Joe, it's Stone. Listen, I just got handed the Jose Robles case."

"Okay, how can I help?"

"I need you to have a look at his sheets."

"*His* sheets?"

"Yeah, from his house. He has some dirty sheets in his linen basket, also the stuff on the bed, pillows, duvet, everything."

"I'm looking for signs of sexual activity?"

"Exactly. And, while you're at it, the same with the bedding from Agnes Shine's place."

"Okay, I'll get a team over there."

"And Joe, I also need you to look for traces of saliva on the glasses. I want to know who drank from them."

"You got it."

I hung up and Dehan said, "We don't know who drank from those glasses?"

"Not for a fact, no. In fact, the outstanding feature about this case is Agnes Shine's absence. Gutierrez assumed she was there because Jose Robles was at her house. Now Frank has added a series of fingerprints to the equation, which we *assume* were made by her. But we don't know for a fact that she made them, do we? And I keep coming back to the same thing: we cannot find even a remote trace of a motive. There is no indication that Agnes and Jose were anything but friends and colleagues."

She screwed up her brow and made a "hmmm" noise. "I don't know, Stone. This may be what in Spanish they call looking for five legs on the cat. The cat's got four legs, not five."

"Yeah, I know, Occam's razor. But frankly, I'm having trouble finding even three legs on this cat. At risk of taxing the metaphor, this cat walks like a duck and quacks like a goose. I keep playing this movie in my head. He's sitting there, in front of the fire, sipping his single malt, reading about batteries, and what happens? The phone rings or somebody knocks at the door."

"It might have been a prior arrangement."

"It might have been. In any case, he leaves his magazine open and he takes his glass to the kitchen." I turned to her. "Did you notice the kitchen? It was spotless. There weren't even dirty plates in the dishwasher. But he leaves the glass by the sink and he walks the two hundred yards to Agnes' house..."

Dehan started talking, staring ahead through the windshield.

"She lets him in, they sit in this very formal way, with the whole sofa between them, sipping a glass of wine each. Then she gets up, goes to the bedroom, takes this gun from somewhere, and shoots him, eight rounds, in a kind of frenzy."

"Yeah, the kind of frenzy where the first shot scores a bull's-eye."

She sighed. "You're right. The rage does seem to come out of left field for no particular reason."

"If I was that mad at someone that I was going to shoot them, I'd confront them on their doorstep. Or if I'd brought them to my house, I wouldn't fix them up with a drink first. The whole setup looks so formal."

She shrugged as she turned onto Boston Road. "Like you said, Stone. They're academics. Maybe they're just weird."

"Maybe. Let's see what Dr. Meigh says."

CHAPTER 3

"They were both a bit weird, to be perfectly honest, Detectives."

Dr. Patricia Meigh was surprisingly small, though her presence was surprisingly large. She sat in her black leather chair, behind her oak desk, like a much bigger woman, and turned her black Parker fountain pen over in her fingers. I frowned.

"Were?"

"Forgive me." She didn't smile. "He was. She, no doubt, continues to be, wherever she is."

Dehan asked, "Weird in what way, exactly?"

She studied her pen a moment, pursing her lips. "You know the big difference between scientists and doctors, or engineers?"

"I have often wondered," I lied.

"For doctors and engineers, it's all about fixing a problem—a *real* problem. The engineer wants to get it built, get it made, put together. The doctor wants to cure her patient, make people well. But for scientists, it's all about proving the hypothesis. They exist in the abstract. They dream up a theory, work out how they can turn the theory into an hypothesis, and they are happy, satisfied, when they can prove the hypothesis is correct. That was Jose and that was Agnes. They both existed—and she presumably continues to exist—in theoretical, hypothetical worlds." She hesitated a moment. "Agnes wasn't strictly a scientist, of course, but a mathematician. Her work was entirely theoretical, in any case."

Dehan gave a small grunt and squinted at Meigh. "That's pretty vague, Dr. Meigh. Can you be more precise?"

"Yes, I can be very precise. They were both completely inept socially. At any kind of social gathering, she would go and stand in a corner and stare, completely unnoticed, while he would butt into other people's conversation and talk incessantly about himself. The man's ego, and his vanity, knew no limits, whereas she is a zero personality. She is a void, an empty space. Quite brilliant, truly, but absolutely no ego." She added, with a touch of bitterness, "They were made for each other."

Dehan looked up from a prolonged study of her thumbs. "So they *were* involved with each other?"

"Oh, good heavens, yes! Involved with each other and, more precisely, involved *in* each other. They went everywhere together, did everything together, forever united in this kind of ghastly, joyless bond. The Jose Robles admiration society, membership of two: him and his slave." A trace of a smile flitted across her face. "I am exaggerating, but not very much."

"Did he talk much about Spain?"

Dehan glanced at me like she thought the question was weird, but Dr. Meigh rolled her eyes and said, "*Incessantly!* Nothing was as good as it was in Spain, especially the food. He was forever moaning about American food, as though all we ever ate was hamburgers. Spanish food was the best in the world. Everything Spanish was the best!"

"Yes, I noticed they both had a lot of Rioja and Ribera del Duero."

"No doubt, whatever that is. Forgive my being blunt, but he was a supreme pain in the ass. And a male chauvinist to go with it: what he used to call the *macho ibérico*. The Iberian macho, a strutting, pompous little . . ." She paused and breathed in noisily through her nose. "I guess I shouldn't really talk about him like that to the cops, huh?"

She smiled and I returned it. "Actually, it is very helpful. We were having some difficulty getting a handle on who they were, and their relationship with each other."

"They were very close," she said. "I have no idea what she saw in him. I am very fond of Agnes. I have known her for a long time and mentored her as an academic. She is a highly intelligent woman, but she has a very weak ego, and he neutralized her completely. I am not a psychologist, but I could see that there was some kind of codependent relationship developing there. It was a shame." She narrowed her eyes and made a kind of claw with her right hand. "He seemed to be *consuming* her. He even rented a house in the same street so he could be close to her and they could come to work together and go home together. I suspect he wanted to control her."

Dehan sat back in her chair. "Were you and she close? Did she ever talk to you about him, them . . ."

She made a dubious face. "She was as close to me as she was to anybody, except Jose, but she never discussed their relationship with me. Whatever they had going on, they were never demonstrative in public. They never hugged or kissed or anything like that." She sat forward suddenly and pointed at her own chest. "*I'd* hug her sometimes, because I felt so goddamn sorry for her! She was hungry for love and affection, you could tell that. But with him it was always me, me, me, and I'm the greatest and Spain is the best damn country in the world. Got on my nerves, I don't mind telling you."

I scratched my cheek and sucked my teeth. "Was he good? As a scientist?"

"Very good. More than very good. He was brilliant. He was on his way to big things."

"You were his boss?"

She smiled like I'd said something quaint. "Doesn't really

work like that. He was conducting research under my supervision, in my department."

"What was the research?"

"I can only tell you in very broad terms, Detective. Obviously it is highly confidential, but in essence, he was conducting research into lithium-ion batteries."

"Next big thing?"

She gave her head a little jerk to the side and raised her eyebrows. "It could lead to a transformation as huge as the Industrial Revolution, or bigger. But I really can't discuss it."

I nodded. "Sure, I understand. And whatever research he conducted would be the property of the university."

"Those are the standard terms of the contract." She frowned. "But I don't see what that can have to do with Agnes killing Jose. They weren't even in the same department. Her work was related to socioeconomic dynamics and the impact of international finance on cultural development."

Dehan spoke suddenly, glancing at me like she agreed with Dr. Meigh and wanted to get the conversation back on track. "You said you were about as close to Agnes as anyone. Have you any idea where she might have gone?"

She shook her head. "I'm sorry, Detective Dehan, none whatsoever. We simply weren't *that* close. I was a friend to her in that I was supportive, but she really never confided in me in any way." She gave a small laugh. "If she has any sense, she's in the Bahamas!"

Dehan grunted and muttered, "Or Goa," then asked, "Was there anyone, besides Jose, that she was close to?"

"No. I don't honestly think she confided in anyone. Jose, maybe, if he were able to listen."

"How about family?"

She smiled. "You're out of luck. She was an only child. Father died when she was a young child, drank himself to death. Mother was an art teacher, if I recall. A rather indolent, negligent woman.

She died a few years back. Agnes inherited the house from her. I am not aware of any other family."

Dehan grunted, then sighed. "How about rivals, Doctor? The way you've described them, they don't sound like very attractive people, but is it possible that Jose had started seeing somebody else?"

She gave a derisive little snort. "It's possible, I suppose. Frankly, I find it hard to believe any woman would go for a man like that, but I am constantly amazed at the specimens some women are attracted to. He may well have been seeing someone else. I am just not aware of it. But please don't get me wrong about Agnes. She is a very sweet person once you get to know her."

I made to stand. "Who has his class now, Doctor?"

"Donald, Donald Hays." She glanced at her watch. "He should be finishing his lecture now, two floors down, in the Goodenough Theater."

I glanced at Dehan. She shrugged and shook her head. I stood.

"Dr. Meigh, thank you for your time. You have been very helpful." She stood, we shook hands, and I opened the door. As Dehan stepped out, I turned to Meigh and asked her, "By the way, which one are you? A doctor or a scientist?"

She looked surprised. "Me? Neither! I'm an academic. All I want is the corner office with the best view, the best parking lot, and a towering reputation."

"Oh." I laughed. "Is that what an academic is? I had often wondered."

I closed the door, and we made our way down two floors in the elevator. After a moment, Dehan frowned at me. "The Goodenough Theater?"

"John Goodenough. He invented the lithium-ion battery."

"Why do you know that?"

I raised an eyebrow. "Why don't you?"

We found Donald Hays leaving the Goodenough Lecture Theater. He was a lean man in his early forties with a big black briefcase, a big, domed head, and balding hair that grew long over his collar. His students streamed about him like a river that has broken its banks, and he was pushing through them like a man trying to escape a flood. He was easy to identify.

"Mr. Hays?" I showed him my badge as the students milled around us. "NYPD. This is Detective Dehan, I am Detective Stone."

He seemed to sag. "Is it about Jose?"

"Yes. Have you somewhere we can go?"

"I have half an hour for lunch. Can we talk in the cafeteria? It's downstairs."

He led us down to the cafeteria at a brisk pace that was hard to keep up with, his head down and his legs moving fast, as though he hoped not to be noticed. As we pushed through the glass doors into the spacious, soulless, self-service canteen, he pointed across the room at a table by the glass wall overlooking Washington Square Village and said, "That's my table. Grab my table. I'll get the coffee. You want coffee?"

We crossed the room, which was hung with a few listless baubles and bits of tinsel, grabbed his table, and sat, watching him load his tray. Dehan dumped her woolen hat on the table and ran her fingers through her hair. "All academics are like this," she pronounced, like she was passing judgment. "They're all crazy. My cousin is a lecturer in the classics. He's the same. Neurotic. Everything is an issue. They're all out of their minds."

"Your cousin is a lecturer in the classics?"

"You never met my family."

"You won't let me."

"I'm afraid you'll judge me."

"That's crazy."

"You see? You're doing it already."

Hays approached with his tray, put it down on the table, and handed out the coffees. As he set about peeling the plastic off his chicken sandwich, he said, "They're fifty cents each."

I gave him a dollar. "How well did you know Jose Robles, Mr. Hays?"

"It's Dr. Hays, and I imagine they have told you already, we were quite close." He bit into his sandwich. Picked up his cup, put it down again, and spoke with his mouth full. "But not close enough to kill him, for God's sake."

He made a face that might have been a smile, tried to sip his coffee, winced, and took another bite from his sandwich.

"Did you socialize?"

He swallowed so he could answer. "Well, I mean, how else would you be close to somebody? Short of moving in together." He gave a small laugh. "And we weren't that close. So we used to go out sometimes. Have a drink and sometimes a meal. And we would talk. That is how you become close, I think."

Dehan leaned her elbows on the table. "Were you close with both of them, or just Jose?"

"I knew Agnes long before Jose came on the scene. We sometimes had lunch together. Like me, she preferred the student cafeteria. At least here people don't stab you in the back . . ." He made a stabbing gesture with his hand, to illustrate. "While you're quietly having your chicken sandwich, as it is today. But it was only when Jose—he liked to be called Pepe, funny story, I'll tell you later—came along, that we started actually *going out*. He was very gregarious. He missed the Spanish nightlife."

She smiled and narrowed her eyes. "Was that just the three of you, or did more people tag along?"

"Mainly it was just us. But sometimes he would go with other people. He was pretty popular. Everybody liked him. He was noisy. People like noisy, I think."

"Noisy?"

He took two bites of his sandwich and nodded. "Mm-hm." He swallowed, reached for his coffee again, but didn't pick it up. "Talked loud. Never stopped."

I scratched my forehead. "Dr. Hays, I need you to think very carefully about this. Is it possible that Jose was seeing another woman, besides Agnes?"

"Why do I have to think carefully about that? It's not a complicated question, Detective. By seeing, I assume you mean having sexual intercourse."

"Yes, that's what I mean. Was he?"

He gave a half smile. "Obviously, I have never been inside his bedroom, which would be a place forbidden to me. But deducing from the signals that people send each other, which they think are secret but are plainly obvious to anyone bothering to watch, I would say that Dr. Robles was involved in a sexual relationship with Ali."

Dehan's eyebrows shot up. "*Ali?*"

Hays swallowed the last of his sandwich with a smirk, picked up his coffee, and sipped. "Forgive my attempt at humor. It is always funny how people assume that Ali is an Arabic man, when she is in fact a Spanish woman. Alicia, abbreviated to Ali. She lectures in Spanish. He used to joke with us that he indulged in intellectual slumming by hanging out with her, because she was only a linguist, not a scientist. But Agnes didn't think it was funny."

Dehan nodded. "Was she jealous?"

"She was too intelligent to be jealous, but she didn't like it."

"She discussed it with you?"

"We both agreed, we didn't know why he wasted his time with her. She had nothing to say—well, she has lots to say, but none of it was of any interest to anybody with any intelligence. But *they* used to talk together. It was more like shouting. They would both shout at the same time, very loudly, and laugh. I think it reminded them of being at home."

"No doubt. Did either Agnes or Jose ever talk to you about guns? Were you aware that either of them owned a gun?"

He gave a smile that was slightly incredulous. "Why would they own a gun? If they were both anti-gun and anti-violence, against the Second Amendment, why would they own a gun?"

I smiled blandly at him. "Could you answer the question please, Dr. Hays?"

"No, neither of them ever talked about *guns*! I have to go. Can I go?"

"Of course, thank you for your help, Doctor."

He didn't say anything. He just stood, picked up his black bag, and walked out of the cafeteria on his fast, anxious legs. Dehan sighed as she watched him go.

"Well, that helped to clarify absolutely nothing."

I nodded. "I wouldn't say absolutely nothing. We have a rough idea of who we are dealing with. They are both very clever, very complicated people, one with a deeply repressed ego, and the other with a hugely inflated one. And we have people with very contradictory opinions of Jose. Dr. Meigh seems not to have liked him at all, and yet, according to Hays, he seems to have been popular."

She scrunched up her hat into a ball and watched it bounce open again. "Possibly he was popular because of the American intellectual's infatuation with all things European."

"Ouch." After a moment, I added, "Ali *is* European, and she seems to have been infatuated with him. Or at least, they sought solace in each other. The allure of the familiar in an alien land."

"How poetic."

"Come on, Dehan. Let's go and do some intellectual slumming and have a chat with this mere linguist."

Scan the QR code below to purchase BLOOD INTO WINE.
Or go to: righthouse.com/blood-into-wine

Printed in Great Britain
by Amazon